For Sally

SHI CHENG

Short Stories from Urban China

Edited by

LIU DING
CAROL YINGHUA LU
and RA PAGE

First published in Great Britain in 2012 by Comma Press
www.commapress.co.uk

'This Moron is Dead' was first published in a collection of the same name [Ci Dai
Yi Si], published by Shanghai Ren Min Chu Ban She (Shanghai People's Press) in
2008. 'Dear Wisdom Teeth' was first published in *Shanghai Literature*, 2002: issue 4.
'Kangkang's Going to Kill that Fucker Zhao Yilu' was first published in *Sparkle*,
2006: issue 8. 'Squatting' was first published in *Writer* magazine, 2006, issue 1.
'Wheels are Round' was first published in *Flower City* magazine,
January 2011.

The moral rights of the authors and translators to be identified as such have been
asserted in accordance with the Copyright Designs and Patents Act 1988.

A CIP catalogue record of this book is available from the British Library.

This collection is entirely a work of fiction. The characters and incidents portrayed
in it are entirely the work of the authors' imagination. The opinions of the authors
are not those of the publisher.

ISBN-10: 190558346X
ISBN-13: 978-1905583461

LOTTERY FUNDED

The publishers gratefully acknowledge assistance from the Arts Council England
North West. This publication in particular has been produced with the support of
the Confucius Institute at the University of Manchester.

Set in Bembo by David Eckersall
Printed and bound in England by MPG Biddles Ltd

CONTENTS

Introduction   ix
Liu Ding, Carol Yinghua Lu & Ra Page

SQUARE MOON   1
Ho Sin Tung
Translated by Petula Parris-Huang

BUT WHAT ABOUT THE RED INDIANS?   17
Cao Kou
Translated by Rachel Henson

KANGKANG'S GONNA KILL THAT FUCKER ZHAO YILU   33
Jie Chen
Translated by Josh Stenberg

RENDEZVOUS AT THE CASTLE HOTEL   45
Yi Sha
Translated by Yu Yan Chen

DEAR WISDOM TOOTH   67
Zhang Zhihao
Translated by Josh Stenberg

CONTENTS

THIS MORON IS DEAD   87
Han Dong
Translated by Nicky Harman

FAMILY SECRETS   99
Ding Liying
Translated by Nicky Harman

WHEELS ARE ROUND   115
Xu Zechen
Translated by Eric Abrahamsen

SQUATTING   139
Diao Dou
Translated by Brendan O'Kane

HOW TO LOOK AT WOMEN   169
Zhu Wen
Translated by Julia Lovell

Authors   203
Translators   206

Introduction

SHI CHENG, OR 'Ten Cities' in English, came into being through a series of chance encounters and unlikely coincidences in various cities in China and the UK. In 1997, one of the editors of this book, Liu Ding, an aspiring artist who dropped out of academia to pursue an independent practice, met Han Dong, a poet and writer who for years had followed his own path, refusing to succumb to the orthodoxies of style and subject preferred by the official Chinese Writers' Association (an organisation that attempts to determine which writers get published and which translated). The two met at a gathering of artists and writers in a bar in Nanjing, and hit it off right away. In the following years, Liu Ding was introduced and exposed to the most active and liberal-thinking group of writers and poets in China, a group he often cites as a crucial influence to the formation of his artistic career. During those years, Liu Ding became extensively familiar with the writings of this circle and was invited by Han Dong to edit the art section of what would become an influential literature magazine, *Furong*, where Han Dong was himself editor-in-chief.

In May 2010, the three editors of this book met after a talk that Carol Yinghua Lu, now Liu Ding's curatorial partner, gave as part of their joint residency at Manchester's Chinese Arts Centre. The talk was about a number of self-driven artistic and literary practices in China. One of these practices was *They*, an underground publishing project set up to give voice to poets and critics, which ran from 1984 to 1994. The initiator of *They* was Han Dong. Together with like-minded friends, Han Dong created a journal that became a rare and important platform for writers and poets to be published outside of the official system, before the opportunities for self-publishing arrived with the internet.

The three of us went out for a drink on the night of a lunar eclipse in Manchester, after which Ra Page took us to the Comma Press office, on the second floor of an artist-run space, MadLab. There, Page went through boxes of books to show us various samples of Comma's output, which included collections of linked or themed short stories, showcases of new writers' work, single-author collections, as well as anthologies of specially translated city-based stories from Europe and the Middle East. In a way, each of Comma's compilations resembled a curatorial project, just as many of Liu and Lu's curatorial projects resemble an anthology, where a range of contributors is invited to address a certain interest or issue in an attempt to broaden and enrich our understanding of it.

Two days after this meeting, the three of us would run into each other again at the annual book fair for not-for-profit publishing houses in Manchester's St Ann's Square. There, Ra Page donned a green Chinese Red Army hat, hanging out at the festive event, which he and a few friends ran to support and encourage independent, non-commercial publishing initiatives in the North of England.

In early November 2012, Page got in touch with Liu and Lu by email, explaining that he had long wanted to publish Chinese short fiction in translation, and asking if Liu and Lu would like to be co-editors of an anthology of city-based stories. It was without a moment of hesitation that Liu and Lu accepted the challenge; despite the project being outside their normal visual arts practice, it was close to their curatorial hearts in many other ways.

Over the following months, the three went on a joint venture, searching for stories set in various cities all over China. Recommendations came through friends, translators, colleagues and respected professionals. Through numerous emails and telephone conversations, we made the final selection of ten stories from dozens of suggested texts, to reflect the diversity of styles, perspectives, and storylines, as well as, of course, settings. The ten authors gathered here represent some of the most important writers born in the 1960s and the 1970s, two generations of writers that are, critically if not commercially, defining the literary scene in China. Quite a number of them have switched from writing poetry to fiction, a phenomenon peculiar to their generation. Owing to the lack of general support and public attention given to poetry, many have resolved to further their craft and explore new forms through fiction, in part to be more accessible to a wider audience. As a group, these stories also tend to favour a more colloquial prose style in order to tell the stories of everyday characters, set in ordinary Chinese cities. And just like the unlikely set of meetings that brought this book's editors together, the characters within these stories follow their own version of Brownian Motion, a seemingly arbitrary trajectory of collisions and ricochets – those random encounters that often define the urban narrative. The order of the stories in this book follows a northbound direction from the southern cities – Hong Kong, Guangzhou, Chengdu – zigzagging through mid-country cities such as Wuhan, Nanjing, Xi'an, Shanghai all the way to Beijing, Shenyang and eventually the ice-cold Harbin.

In these stories, the cities come alive and provide glimpses into some of the more dazzling and absurd contradictions that the last three decades have brought with them. We see the full spectrum of challenges currently facing Chinese cities: from the influx of rural populations caught up in the inexorable tide of urbanization (as in Cao Kou's story, set in the manufacturing powerhouse that is Guangzhou), to the changing nature of China's middle classes and the 'gentrification of government' (brilliantly parodied in Diao Dou's Shenyang story); from the loss of a sense of community (in Han Dong's Nanjing story) to the frustrated and sometimes ludicrous fetishization of material possessions (Xu Zechen's Beijing story). Comedy and an eye for the absurd unite many of the stories here; other themes come to the surface as well. Western readers might be surprised, for instance, by quite how much store is still set by education as a means for characters to climb above their station, and consequently how many of them are haunted by early rejections or failings within the education system.

In every case, these stories offer a particularly Chinese response to the challenges of urban life. But while the landscapes, details, noises and smells are all explicitly Chinese in nature, the emotions that underpin them – the humanity, the desires and anxieties of each and every character – are quite universal. Their emotions may be married to specific circumstances, but paradoxically, it is this very specificity that infuses the stories with authenticity; an authenticity that can be recognised and understood by anyone, anywhere in the world. As Diao Dou writes in his story set in the northern Chinese city of Shenyang, 'The above shouldn't be taken to reflect the primary characteristics of summer nights in our city – merely a single aspect, incidental, a footnote to a greater whole. In principle, I believe [...] our city at the macro level is hardly different from Paris or Warsaw, Pyongyang or London, Tokyo or Beijing, Baghdad or Port-au-Prince, Canberra or Kabul, Sarajevo or Caracas, Addis Ababa or Buenos Aires.'

LD, CYL, RP, March 2012

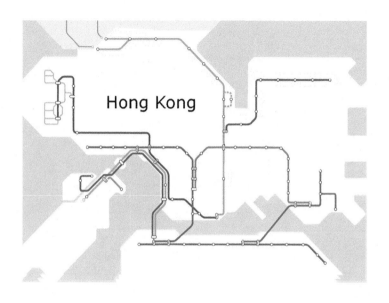
Hong Kong

Square Moon

Ho Sin Tung

Translated by Petula Parris-Huang

SHE LEAVES HIS house for the first time but not the last. A bus approaches, which she boards hastily, the touch of that icy-cold hand still lingering on her shoulder. She sits by the window and watches as the bus enters a dark tunnel. It feels as though they are driving straight into the cavernous throat of some strange creature. In the darkness, she can see her reflection in the windowpane; there is also a foreigner sitting not far behind her.

Meeting foreigners is part of her job. She always makes an effort to greet them with a few polite words and then, in that awkward moment while she is waiting for them to turn around and walk away, they always seem to ask her the same question: 'Where do you live?'

'Sheung Shui,' she tells them, occasionally adding how it is located in the very north of Hong Kong.

But that wasn't what *he* asked when they first met. She was sitting on duty in the gallery that morning and, with so few customers about, was reading a novel by Louis-Ferdinand Céline. The edition was a translation from a Taiwanese publisher and had a painting by Caspar David Friedrich on the cover. The picture showed a man standing with his back to the reader, staring defiantly out into the distance – and was the exact image of what she would come to imagine Céline

1

to look like. She was still only about one-fifth of her way through the novel at this point, and little did she know how long it would take to rid herself of the story. Little did she know that its rusty hooks were already clawing their way into her flesh, one by one.

It was at this moment that he walked in, and it was already too late to stop him. She quickly stuffed the book under the counter and said hello, while he signaled to her that he was happy to look around by himself. She nodded and sat back down, but was too scared to take the book out again, as if reading was some terribly shameful act. He was taking forever to look at the paintings and so, feeling bored, she started to weigh him up. He was somewhere in his fifties or sixties – green eyes, grey hair, shirt and jeans. Not a lot different to all of the other Western men walking around Central.

He walked over to the counter, and she stood up straight with her hands clasped behind her back as she watched him leaf his way through the exhibition catalogue and price list. She could tell from the way he turned each page that he was an extremely sensitive person, but she also detected a hint of neurosis in those delicate movements. Then, as his hands left the pages and he took off his glasses, her line of vision followed until she was looking straight at him. 'You know what kind of person Céline was, don't you?' he said.

It took a moment for her to understand what he meant.

'You know that he was a ****ist, don't you?'

The bus exits the tunnel and sunlight falls onto the square of newspaper on her lap. The paper is thin, like a scrap of rubbish. And the sunlight? The sunlight is composed of the last few golden rays that shine out before the sky turns black. The foreigner on the bus is sleeping deeply, quite undisturbed by the light. She has left his house and entered into darkness, only to continue to an even darker place. On one particular day, about six months earlier, it had seemed that he wanted to get closer, but also that he didn't. Either way, they were already close. With a sudden impulse to be the first to act, she had turned her face away from him, her body following until she was facing entirely the opposite direction. She did not stop to think what might happen to be in that direction.

In front of her was a poster for a film, consecrated in the night-time by the glow of a spotlight. 'Wow, that's big,' she thought to herself.

But later it would end up being so small.

He never left his business card that day, in the gallery, but he did ask for hers. Her business card was very much like her job – completely void of any personality. She had only ever chosen to study art because the entrance grades were so low, and, during high school, she found it ridiculous that people complimented her on her drawing when all she had done was design some pictures for the classroom noticeboard or add a few doodles to a poster. Still, she would smile back at her classmates while thinking to herself, 'Ah, your worlds and mine, they are just so very small…' By the time she entered university, her fellow students were already busy trying to establish themselves as artists, struggling to get signed up with art galleries or hold exhibitions at a particularly reputable venue. She, on the other hand, decided from very early on that she would major in art administration. She extracted herself from the chaos of the studio, where night was barely distinguishable from day, and decided to take courses in art history and management instead.

She had a boyfriend at the time, but it is not an experience worth dwelling on, having smashed her entire being to pieces. Later on, after picking up the fragments of her broken flesh and bone, she graduated and started work at the gallery. She was a quick worker, and the gallery was not a particularly famous one, only ever holding one exhibition every couple of months. This left her with a lot of free time, which, provided her boss was away and there were no customers, she spent reading novels. Her daily commute from

Sheung Shui to Central took almost one and a half hours each way, and so she usually clocked up a further three hours reading in the time that she was transporting her body back and forth. She had once considered herself lucky to be able to catch the MTR at Sheung Shui. So few passengers boarded the train at Lo Wu that there were still plenty of empty seats by the time it reached her – whereas just one stop further down the line, at Fanling, it was suddenly standing room only. But, of course, that was back in the days when there weren't so many people coming down from the mainland. That was back when the Chinese renminbi was still cheap.

Now, everything was different. Flocks of mainlanders crammed their way into the station at Sheung Shui and she hated her home more and more.

The second time they met was in a restaurant near the gallery. She was already sitting down when he walked in, having ordered braised beef with noodles. Recognising her, he nodded in her direction, chose a seat nearby and attempted to order his meal in exceptionally bad Cantonese. Despite the fact that the female restaurant owner couldn't understand a word he was saying, he managed to stay calm and, seen from a distance, it almost looked as though he was trying to teach the owner new words. She walked over to give them a hand. He ordered bitter melon with roast pork and rice, after which she sat down to eat with him at the same table. At last, he asked her where she lived, and for a change he actually knew where Sheung Shui was. She was very surprised at his choice of meal and couldn't help commenting on how 'local' it was – not what most foreigners would order at all. He asked her how old she was, and she told him that she was twenty-five. He told her that he'd been living in Hong Kong for thirty years already, which made him more 'Hong Kong' than she was! So there was really nothing surprising about his choice. He delivered his words with a smile – the sort of smile that she would use with her classmates.

Feeling embarrassed, all she could think of was to ask him where he lived. She expected him to say one of the stops on the blue MTR line, but instead he hesitated for a moment before simply stating that he lived on 'Hong Kong Island'. His answer was deliberately vague, but it was thanks to his vagueness that they quickly became friends. For how could they have continued had he been any more earnest?

He often arranged to meet her for lunch and sometimes emailed her in the evenings. He was single, lived alone, and had lots and lots of time on his hands. Sometimes, he became so engrossed in something that he could hardly pull himself away from it. He was almost as old as her father, but there was nothing that they couldn't talk about. In fact, he was a very open and honest person – not at all as quirky as she had first thought. Before long, she had started to forget how to say certain words in Chinese.

It was only when their conversations turned to his home that he would suddenly seem lost for words. Similarly, whenever they parted, he always seemed to take a different route home. Nevertheless, she did manage to uncover a few clues, such as when she mentioned a community art project in Sham Shui Po and he told her how he had lived there on his arrival to Hong Kong. He remarked what a nice place it was, at which point she laughed and told him about when she had had to study a pile of local police reports for one of her research projects. 'It turns out that all the murderers and rapists like to hide in Sham Shui Po after they commit their crimes,' she told him. 'I never expected it to be one of your old neighbourhoods!' But he didn't laugh.

Another day, when they were walking along a street in Central, several of the shopkeepers and passers-by started to say hello to him. As they passed each one, he recounted that particular individual's story and, when she asked him how he knew so much, he replied perfectly innocently that this was where his house was. He pointed to his house, which was painted blue. It was at that moment that her memory split open, although of course she did not know it at the time.

There was nothing particularly striking about the house. It was like a child, your average child – a little withdrawn, perhaps, and not especially attractive. You think to yourself, 'Yes, it's just that kind of child.'

When they parted that day, he mentioned that he would be taking the bus home. He had said that the house was his, but he didn't say that he lived there. Is that how one was supposed to interpret his words? It was that evening, at the bus stop, that she turned away from him and saw that enormous poster.

Here, on the bus, she is clutching a square of newspaper with an advert for the very same film. The advert would have once occupied a full-page spread but, by now, the box office statistics, awards, commendations and reviews have already long faded from view. It occurs to her how the advert is just as small as she is, although of course she was never that big.

Another day, when they were in Mong Kok, he told her that he was planning to walk home. It was the first time that he had ever mentioned going home on foot, and so she decided to follow him – something that, in Mong Kok, was not an especially difficult thing to do. The street was so busy that she simply walked out in the open behind him, though making a point of leaving a wide enough gap between them. He turned away from the main street and into an alleyway, where he proceeded to walk up a flight of steps under a sign for the 'Hotel Spain'.

She assumed that he was going to visit a prostitute, but was not repulsed in anyway. He was single, after all. Moreover, the idea of a Western man paying for the services of an Oriental woman was, in reality, not that difficult to accept. On the contrary, the sheer crassness of this very image was already deeply embedded in the locals' psyche.

She lingered for a while outside the Hotel Spain, before

noticing that there was also a 'Hotel Rome' next door. The two cities stood selling their wares without the slightest distance between them. Without really knowing why, she decided to spend the night at the Hotel Rome. It was the first time that she had ever visited one of Hong Kong's 'rest hotels', and had always assumed that they existed solely for the purpose of sexual transactions. However, as she completed the registration formalities, she saw that many of the guests came from the mainland and were dragging large suitcases behind them.

Although she had never been to Rome, she knew that it looked nothing like the hotel, which was dilapidated and gaudy. The bathroom floor was tiled with black and white squares and, on the mirror, was a discarded flag[1] that someone must have peeled from their chest a previous Saturday. Seeing a number of short, dark hairs stuck to the quilt, she lay down on the bed without covering herself and started to read. She made a point of reading as slowly as she could, worried that if she reached the end too quickly there would be nothing else to do. Eventually, she finished the book and, as expected, had no other means of occupying herself. She thought that perhaps she could reflect on all of the people who had deserted her and then wallow in the resulting sensation of emptiness and boredom. But it didn't work. Instead, she kept thinking how, although he was in Spain and she was in Rome, they were still close neighbours. Her old school also happened to be in Kowloon Tong, and so most of her classmates lived in the area. But she had never made the type of friend with whom she could walk home from school or arrange to meet in the evening for dessert.

---

1. Saturday is known as 'Flag Day' in Hong Kong, meaning that public fundraising is permitted by the government. Fundraisers take to the streets and stick small stickers to the clothing of anyone donating money to their cause, with these stickers being known as 'flags' in both Cantonese and English.

It was as she was dwelling on this abundant loneliness that the blue house suddenly popped into her mind. She could tell that the house was missing its owner. It made her feel very upset.

The next morning she was late for work and, by the time she arrived, a curator visiting especially from overseas had already phoned to find out why the gallery wasn't open. She duly received a severe dressing down from her boss, who, being in a particularly bad mood due to problems at home, remarked scathingly how only 'artists' had the right to be habitually late. 'It's part of their character,' he told her. 'But you're just a second-rate art graduate who sits here waiting on other artists because you can't be one yourself!' His words left her feeling miserable for the rest of the day. Then, when she arrived home in the evening, her father reprimanded her for not coming home the night before. She lived alone with her father, her mother having died many years earlier, and she considered that, at twenty-five, she was too old to put up with this kind of scolding. She ended up swearing at him, but when she couldn't think of the right word in Chinese, she used an English word to fill in the gap. This sent her father, whose English was far from brilliant, into an uncontrollable rage. He said that he supposed she'd studied all those years just so she could use English to intimidate people? But who had forked out all of that money for her to study in the first place? She couldn't bear to listen to anymore of his rantings and walked straight out of the house.

She called his number and asked whether she could go to Spain to see him.

It took a few moments for him to register, after which followed the embarrassed silence of somebody who has just had his private life thrown open for all the world to see. He could tell from her voice, though, that something was wrong, so he didn't want to get angry. 'OK,' he replied, knowing that he had little choice, 'but tonight I'm in Hawaii.'

The thought of Hawaii conjured up images of sunny

beaches and women swaying in grass skirts, which hardly seemed to fit with the soap opera-esque scene of her storming out of her home. All the same, she decided to follow his directions to the hotel. It was located inside Tsim Sha Tsui's Chungking Mansions.

He was waiting for her in front of the elevator, his face appearing as pale as a corpse under the fluorescent tube lighting and rendering him extremely unattractive. Reality began to dawn upon her. She had come, in the middle of the night, to meet someone in this sort of place. Was everything that was destined to happen about to happen? Why did it have to be right then, under that kind of light, with her witnessing him in all his paleness...? She started to recoil.

It was almost as if he could read her thoughts. 'Go to sleep, kid,' he told her. 'You're tired.'

It was true that she was only a child. She followed him into the hotel, which was actually nothing more than a partitioned-off unit in the centre of the building and looked even more rundown than Rome. She washed herself somewhat indifferently in the simple bathroom, foregoing her usual routine of cleansing, toning and moisturising her face or conditioning her hair. There is a reason that makes a woman less carefree than a man, and that is that the baggage she carries is both heavier and more manifold. Her belongings may appear trivial, but they are often unbearably cumbersome.

She returned to the bedroom to find him sat reading on the room's one and only bed. She sat beside the bed and dried her hair with a towel, attempting to fathom the unfathomable. When she turned back towards him, she saw that he had stopped reading and was watching her instead. 'Why don't you ever go home?' she asked.

'Home?' He repeated the word as if it was a stupid question.

'To that blue house,' she added.

She expected this to be the moment that he would let it

all out. It would be a fantastical and deeply moving story. But, instead, he simply said, 'I do go home. I go home once a week to fetch clean clothes.'

She was more than a little disappointed by his answer. In her view, that lonely house was supposed to be more like Duras' Indochina or Magnani's Pontito – far out of reach, but never far from mind. But no, all it took was dirty clothes to draw him back.

Although she was by nature a very practical person, after falling asleep and waking up again, she had a hugely impractical thought – she would travel the world with him.

It was hardly a spur of the moment decision. Her father had paid her way through university and duly held very high expectations for her. But unlike most residents in the city, who thought that artists only ever earned money once they were dead, her father had always made a point of following art-related news for his art student daughter. He had read about speculators buying up artworks for astronomical prices, and was therefore deeply disappointed that, rather than becoming an artist, his daughter had settled for a low-ranking administrative post in an art gallery. The fact that he often ridiculed her about this made theirs an even more peculiar situation. Most parents in Hong Kong would have viewed an administrative position as a stable career choice, and the idea of 'becoming an artist' as being highly unrealistic. But, in this particular case, this non-mainstream father had found himself a very mainstream daughter. His daughter hoped that her leaving home for a few days would make him realise just how far he had driven her. In any case, her daily three-hour commute had left her drained, and she resented having such a huge chunk of her life taken up with the ritual of her transporting herself from north to south and back again. True, she probably read a few more books than other people, and she was probably also better at waiting than most. But apart from that she had nothing.

He said that they would stay in Hawaii for a few days

and then, the next week, they would go to Venice.

After that, they went to New York, Paris and San Diego. The lands of milk and honey. Although he always treated her like a child, they became very, very close.

She presses the red stop button on the bus. The foreigner has already gone, and the newspaper in her hands has grown soggy from her sweat, a veritable piece of rubbish. She kneads her shoulder, which still feels cold, leaving a set of black fingerprints as she does so. It is already dark outside.

Times had been good. One night, she dreamed that lots of women were stood screaming on top of a dark hill, before then waking to find herself drenched in sweat. She touched herself below and brought her hand back to study it. Her fingertips were wet and glistening. Just like Moses, as he traveled to a place far away from his people and closer to God, her face glowed. She then discovered that he was watching her, like a snake in the darkness.

Finally, in Osaka, after washing and drying herself so that she was perfectly clean, she leant forward to kiss him. She told herself that she was young and he was old. Nothing could go wrong, as long as she was willing.

But he pushed her away, saying, 'There's something a bit strange about that house.'

How completely random! What did any of this have to do with the house? She had assumed that his reason for their 'traveling around' was the same as hers – to find an escape from the monotony of daily life.

'I often see a woman waiting in the corner, like an apparition,' he said.

She froze. That wasn't something you would describe as a 'bit strange' – it was quite off the scale of weirdness. She recalled that the blue house was on Tai Ping Shan Street in Sheung Wan. Lots of people had died in the area, indeed it was known to be haunted. A drop of water fell from her hair onto her chest, causing her to shiver. She could see that something was troubling him, but he also seemed calm. 'Aren't you scared?' she asked.

Rather than replying, he sank deep into thought and stayed there. It reminded her of when he had avoided telling her exactly where he lived. 'Anyway, what does this have to do with us?' she asked.

'Her,' he replied.

He didn't say anymore, but she thought she understood, and she returned home the very next day.

There was a festival one month later, during which he invited her to watch the fireworks by the seafront. The crowds were heaving, and he told her not to stop but to keep walking. She thought to herself how ludicrous the array of different lighting along the road looked. There were also signs on the railings warning people that climbing was forbidden. But if someone had really wanted to climb the railings, then what did such signs matter? It was just like he was always telling her to 'come, come closer...'

Then, right there in the place where he had told her not to stop, he said that he didn't want his house anymore.

She thought that hearing this would make her happy, but it didn't. Instead of thinking about the woman in the house, she just thought about how it was just a house – more innocent than a puppy. It was simply somewhere where he was not. It harboured no evil intentions and all it had was him. It had never hurt anybody.

'Then your house will remember you forever,' she said, despairingly.

He looked straight into her eyes. 'Great,' he said. 'So why don't I abandon you tomorrow, so that you also remember me forever?'

She allowed him to gaze inside her. With a life so finite, privacy to her seemed as superfluous as an elaborate golden key. What was the point of locking oneself away within the confines of a tiny spinning top when, at the end of the day, even the most determined among us is little different to a pot plant, waiting desperately to be watered?

'Go home,' she said to him. 'Your house is weeping, it misses you.'

That was the last time they met. Her father started speaking to her again and she carried on working at the gallery as before. Then, earlier today, she received a text from him inviting her to his home. She followed the nameplate to his house, found the door unlocked and walked in to see him hanging there. But she did not even feel that shocked. The house was just as she expected, full of the signs of life, but imbued with a profound sense of emptiness despite the clutter. The blue house had no more tears to shed. It was not young anymore; it was no longer a child.

She saw the day's newspaper on the table, and in it spotted the advertisement for the film. It had already shrunk in size. It had been waiting for her all along.

'I guess I might as well go and watch it.'

Just at she was thinking this, she felt a hand press down on her shoulder. The hand was steady and cold. It was the hand of a woman.

She shrugged the hand off and, without looking back, walked straight out of the building – which is how she came to be here, getting off the bus and walking into a department store. Flocks of young couples crowd around restaurant fronts waiting for their table numbers to be called, fragments of personal letters are displayed on electronic display boards, and the strains of alternating piano tunes play out in the background, one after another. She heads upwards, rising from one floor to the next, until she is so high that it occurs to her that anybody leaning against the glass barrier in the store's centre could easily fall crashing to the floor below.

'I know that he's a ****ist,' she says to herself.

She reaches the cinema entrance and is just in time for the film, but on buying a ticket she can hardly recognize her own voice. The film has been playing for so long that today is the last showing and she has the entire screen to herself. An usher rips her ticket as she stands waiting outside the curtain. The city is crumbling. It is but a shadow of its former self.

A voice booms out from inside the curtain—

'Someone is coming.'

But What About the Red Indians?

Cao Kou

Translated by Rachel Henson

In the spring of 2008 there was a devastating earthquake in Sichuan, Zhao Qinghe lost his job, and then something really strange happened.

After an evening drinking with friends alongside Wuyang Newtown's infamous reeking creek, he went back to his flat (rented of course) and fell instantly asleep. As usual, he woke up thirsty in the middle of the night and climbed out of bed to get a drink of water. He was in the kitchen, just about to put the light on and turn on the tap, when he realised that there was someone standing there right in front of him: a tall and incredibly thin woman. Afterwards he wasn't sure it had been a woman. As far as he could tell, this person had no breasts, so there was no way it could have been a woman, right?

'Maybe she was flat-chested,' said a friend, laughing.

'I don't know why you're laughing,' said Zhao Qinghe quite seriously. 'It was really creepy, even more so now I come to think about it.'

'You didn't think so at the time?' said the friend.

'Yeah, it's funny, I wasn't scared at the time, not in the least,' said Zhao Qinghe.

'Maybe because you thought it was a woman?'

Zhao Qinghe nodded but then shook his head.

They finally decided that it must have been a hallucination. I mean, there's no such thing as ghosts and anyway, it was the only explanation Zhao Qinghe could live with so he just had to go with it. But a few days later, something else happened.

He had decided to go and talk to his landlord in the hope of persuading him to give him more time to pay the rent. In the normal scheme of things this wouldn't have been possible. The contract said he should transfer the money into his account every month and if there was a problem, the agent would deal with it. Landlord and tenant wouldn't usually have any contact apart from knowing each other's names. But when he'd first rented the flat, the agent had once taken him to the landlord's house, which was about five stops away on the bus. There was a foot massage place there that Zhao Qinghe used to go to a lot, to the extent of eventually having his declaration of love turned down by the regular foot massage girl. Of course this was all past history and, according to Zhao Qinghe, the less said about it the better.

When he got on the bus there was an empty seat waiting for him but just as he was about to sit down, he was beaten to it by the great lump of lard behind him whose massive great behind completely sealed up the seat space. It was just depressing. Okay, he thought, so I've let him sit down, but why does he have to be so fat? I mean a backside that big is simply unjustifiable. He clutched the hand-grip, frowning. Just then, a young girl inadvertently brushed her breast against his elbow as she went past. He felt the shape of it so precisely, the touch so intensely – I mean, as you've probably realised, Zhao Qinghe was close on becoming a thirty-year-old virgin. Whenever a girl did that kind of thing he would always check her out self-consciously. But it was no use. There were three girls standing there behind him and he couldn't tell which one of them it had been.

It was really hot. No one was wearing that much. If everyone had stripped completely naked and put their clothes in a heap, it wouldn't have amounted to a pimple. Zhao Qinghe had to move away and take some deep breaths to calm down. The air inside the bus was foul and breathing deeply was against all common sense, but at least it distracted his attention. He looked out of the window. It hadn't rained for a good few days. The traffic careering past stirred up the road dust. The sun was the colour of a bad quality soft drink.

The bus had stopped at a red light and looking through the window he saw a middle-aged couple standing on the grass verge by the side of the road. Their clothes were old-fashioned and unusually clean and smart so it wasn't hard to tell they were from the countryside. They were probably conventional villagers unfamiliar with a city like Guangzhou. At most, their knowledge of the city would go as far as a map bought from the coach station. The man could have been a village bookkeeper or salesman who had been to the city years ago on business, and back then, as a direct result of his travel experience and status in the village, he had got this probably good-looking village maiden to marry him (the middle-aged woman he could see now). Before this return trip he had perhaps boasted of the city to his wife - its famous sites and street food, its avenues and alleyways - as if boasting of the family jewels, but when they actually got here he was just embarrassed and bewildered at how different everything was from how he remembered. His memories had become fantasies. The reality was that he had brought his wife here only to lose them both in this forsaken corner of the city, this roadside verge smothered in dust, this half-dead bit of grass.

What were they doing there? Zhao Qinghe took advantage of the finite time waiting at the red light to look at them in detail. The woman was vomiting. Filth, pouring from the largest cavity in her bright clean face, spurted reluctantly out of her. It probably consisted of rice porridge and soya paste from breakfast at home and a bread and mineral water midday meal on the journey. It looked as if they had just got off the coach and the wife was suffering from severe travel sickness. The desperately concerned husband kept patting her on the back, hoping to make her feel better, but as she vomited what remained in her gut, she shrugged off his constant patting with an expression of irritation, her hand still clutching an embroidered handkerchief. The patting wasn't having the miraculous effect he hoped for. We should all take note. You're not going to help anyone, even your bosom companion, just by wishing it.

The lights changed to green, the bus started off, the middle-aged couple receded further and further away until they disappeared through the very last window at the back of the bus.

Zhao Qinghe guessed that they had come to see their son. Maybe he was at college in the city or was working in one of those so-called sweatshops somewhere in Huadu District. Yes, they had probably come for a visit. He remembered his father coming for a visit once too, standing by a green rubbish bin outside the college gate carrying a scruffy snakeskin bag waiting for his son to show up. Trouble was his son didn't want to come out. Whenever Zhao Qinghe thought of it he felt a stab of pain in his gut. Father, what are you doing now? Still digging in the dirt like a dog? To be honest, everything Zhao Qinghe saw, smelt or felt on the way to his landlord's had a profound effect on his state of mind, and he was in a terrible state, as bad as it gets.

When it gets as bad as that there's a chance things will change for the better. Trouble was, as it turned out, Zhao Qinghe's landlord wasn't at home. The whole journey had been a complete waste of time. Of course he should have got in touch over the phone. They could have discussed the whole thing or arranged a time to meet – much better than having a wasted journey. But it was as if he hadn't made this phone call on purpose, as a way of showing his sincerity, in order to gain the landlord's sympathy and therefore generosity and to demonstrate just how desperate he was.

His mood sunk to a new low. He began to walk back. Take note, he set off walking, he didn't get on the bus. Why? Who knows? We could surmise that he wanted to meet the middle-aged couple and appeal to them each in turn: 'Mum! Dad!' and then yell 'Get out of my sight!' He walked about the distance of two stops until he came to the place where they had stood. Of course they were nowhere to be found. The vomit was still there. Zhao Qinghe couldn't help having a closer look. He only glanced at it quickly but it was enough to make him feel terrible.

After he had gone past that place, he felt he just couldn't go on anymore. He noticed some low-rise shacks along the side of the road that had been converted into shops. Some did household decorating or put credit onto mobile phones. Some had black tables offering passers-by roast goose lunch boxes. There were a lot of fruit stalls. The stink of durian fruit was overpowering. There were the usual kiosks selling cigarettes, alcohol, soft drinks and junk food. According to the newspapers, a few people died from eating this food of uncertain origin every year. Healthy or unhealthy, for some, it was all they had. So it wasn't the food itself, or where it came from that really mattered, but your circumstance, your fate, whether you deserved it or not.

Zhao Qinghe noticed that one of the kiosks had a couple of chairs that looked a bit cleaner than the ones at the snack stall, so he walked over and sat down.

'Just having a rest,' he said to the stallholder who was sitting opposite, behind the square glass counter. The stallholder didn't reply, just lifted his head and looked at Zhao Qinghe and then looked down again, revealing each one of his facial features as he did so. They were completely unremarkable, the sort you would easily forget. Maybe he was a native of Canton or Guangxi or maybe he was Hakka; I mean if you said he was from somewhere round about Hunan, no one would argue. Zhao Qinghe couldn't help standing up and peering in to have another look, just to make sure.

'Can I help you?' The stallholder stood up. His accent didn't offer a clue to where he was from either. Zhao Qinghe sat down at once, maybe as a way of making it clear that he didn't want to buy anything and as a hint to the stallholder to sit back down as well. But he was too late.

'Can I help you?' The stallholder asked once more.

'Oh,' said Zhao Qinghe, 'I'm sorry, I don't want anything, thank you.'

'You don't want anything,' repeated the stallholder disappointedly, and began to sink back down slowly, eventually reaching a sitting position. Zhao Qinghe couldn't help sighing in relief and gave him a little smile. This made him stand up again.

'Look, do you want anything or not?' The stallholder's voice was noticeably shriller.

'I don't want anything, thank you,' said Zhao Qinghe frankly, and then added: 'Really.'

'So what are you doing?' asked the stallholder.

'Nothing.'

The stallholder probably wanted to say: 'Then why do you keep looking at me?' But that wasn't the sort of thing a normal person would ask on this abnormal evening, so instead he said: 'If you don't want to buy anything then you'd better leave.'

'I'm just having a rest,' said Zhao Qinghe. 'I'm tired of walking. Am I interfering with your business? If I am then I'll go at once.' He even made as if to get up.

'Oh.' The stallholder didn't respond further. Nor did he sit down again. He stared blankly without malice or goodwill at the traffic going past, somehow echoing the constant blank gaze of his kiosk. Then, as if he had just remembered something, he turned and went further inside, one hand lifting the curtain. You wouldn't have guessed there could be any more space inside. Maybe a bed or a stove, or a woman lying on the bed, her thigh sticking out from under the quilt. As he went inside he hesitated and glanced back at Zhao Qinghe. Zhao Qinghe evaded his gaze at once. He suddenly felt bad – there was something wrong about this whole business. Why should he scrutinize the stallholder's every move?

The stallholder came out again really quickly, checked the goods that could be easily lifted from the counter and then looked at Zhao Qinghe to see whether any part of him looked lumpy. Zhao Qinghe understood what he was up to. He stood up and even went as far as to shake himself out in an exaggerated manner. Nothing fell out. Then he said: 'Thanks. I'm off now.'

He hadn't gone far when he heard the stallholder behind him say: 'Thanks for what?'

Zhao Qinghe stopped and turned, and making an effort to be friendly, said: 'Nothing really. Thank you for letting me sit down for a while.'

'Oh.' The stallholder's head withdrew. Zhao Qinghe had no choice but to continue on his way. If he carried on walking, he'd probably get all the way home before dark, but for some reason the more he walked, the more he was filled with despair. As a way of halting this downward spin he turned back and appeared again in front of the kiosk.

'You again?' said the stallholder in surprise.

'Yes,' said Zhao Qinghe with a forced smile that seemed to imbue the air with pain. 'I forgot just now. I'd like a pack of cigarettes.'

'I thought so.' The stallholder brightened up: 'Which kind?'

'Double Happiness, Red. How much is that?'

'Seven kuai.'

'Oh, right.'

Zhao Qinghe paid for the cigarettes and left.

'Bye then.'

'Bye.'

He ripped open the cigarettes as he walked and got one out to smoke. The evening looked stormy, or maybe it was the draft caused by the high-speed traffic that made him feel that something about the cigarette was wrong. He started to think about the ways you can tell between a fake and a real one. Things like if the stem is too soft, or if the paper around the filter is loose, or if the ash is very dark and hard. The more he thought about it, the more it seemed so. The ash didn't look very white or even, in any case.

A stab of humiliation seared right through him. He appeared outside the kiosk for the third time.

'Hey! These are fakes!' said Zhao Qinghe, and he flung the pack onto the counter with such force that it nearly slid right over and off the other side.

'Don't talk rubbish,' said the owner, his face hardening as he grasped what was happening. 'I have never sold fakes.'

'Crap! This pack's fake.'

'Oh, I can't be bothered with you.' The owner pushed the pack away, then sat on that chair of his and looked away, his leg beginning to judder. This time, Zhao Qinghe noticed that it was a canvas deck chair. It even had a cushion. The stallholder certainly knew how to look after himself. The juddering leg made Zhao Qinghe's voice shake a bit.

'Give me another pack.'

True to his word, the owner carried on ignoring him.

'Didn't you hear me? What's the point of selling fakes?'

'What do you mean, fakes? Why should they be?' The stallholder couldn't help standing up. 'They're not fakes just because you say they are.'

'For fuck's sake, of course I can tell the difference. I've smoked quite a few Double Happiness Reds in my time.'

'You've got no idea. I repeat, I've never in my life sold fake cigarettes. And how about keeping your language clean, young man.'

'Bullshit! They're fake and always will be. What's it to you, anyway. I can talk how I like.'

'Get out of it you little prick!' howled the stallholder.

'You fucker!' Zhao Qinghe cursed him and hit out but couldn't reach over the counter so he grabbed anything within reach and began to smash it up.

The owner came right out of his kiosk with a stick he'd reached for from somewhere behind the counter. He didn't actually hit Zhao Qinghe, just shook the stick at him to warn him off, but Zhao Qinghe didn't get that. He bent down swiftly and picked up a lump of rock.

It's tired me out, writing up to this point. Maybe I find it hard kicking the habit of making stuff up but I assure you that this is all true. My friend Li Ruiqiang, who lives in Guangzhou, told me about it personally. He and Zhao Qinghe were classmates – they're from the same place – You County in Hunan. When Li Ruiqiang told me this story about Zhao Qinghe, he also told me some other stuff about him. As it's not my story, I'm not really going to do it justice, so I've decided to tell it in Li Ruiqiang's voice from now on in.

I remember when we were at high school it was all because of a girl in our class called Gao Jing that we didn't get into university. Gao Jing got in, went to Beijing, stayed there after graduation and then I heard that she got married to someone abroad. The last time we saw her was on the last day of the uni entrance exams. I wasn't in the same room as her, but Zhao Qinghe was. He said when he caught sight of the little white vest inside her short-sleeved shirt it was very tight. Oh so tight.

Anyway, me and Zhao Qinghe had to stay on and repeat a year – the so-called fourth year. We didn't have our lessons at school. Instead, the school had rented a farm building in the middle of some fields that were originally used for threshing and drying during the time of collective farms. The third-year teachers took it in turns to bike out there from school to give us lessons. We only went to school for practicals. So, whether the teachers came out to us or we went to school for experiments, we always had to go through a wheat field and past a stream – in other words, across a certain bridge. It was a concrete arched bridge built in 1978, as I remember, with a five-pointed star on each of the pillars and a few Mao quotations still visible on the concrete panels between the railings. I can't remember which ones. There was also some stuff scribbled by school kids. Things like *I fucked XXX's mum* scrawled in chalk, lime or brick dust. Underneath, down below the bridge, there was even more scope and the content got even more interesting. Me and Zhao Qinghe wrote a lot of things on those concrete walls. He wrote *I want to fuck Gao Jing* and so, of course, did I.

We often hung out under the bridge skipping class. Certainly, all through the third year, especially in the last term and, it goes without saying, a lot during the so-called fourth year. Why should we go to class? Truly, to us, at the time, the future was dark. All we saw was endless lessons and schoolwork. Going to university seemed completely hopeless. I often used to sigh, just like I do now, but Zhao Qinghe wasn't like that. I knew him very well. He was different. He still sighed though, I heard him.

So we endured another year, hiding under the bridge. The exams came round again, the scores, the lowest acceptable mark. I got into Sun Yat-sen University against all expectations. And, as expected, Zhao Qinghe didn't pass. He had to repeat the whole year again - the so-called fifth year. I don't know how he got by that year, even though we wrote to each other. You know, students who have just left home all have this thing about writing letters. There was no internet so getting letters was brilliant. It was just great. Makes me quite sentimental to think of it. But after a while even writing letters gets boring, especially with someone like Zhao Qinghe. He just wasn't much fun. His letters were dull and none of them were very long.

Then I got a girlfriend at university and slept with her not long after. I wrote excitedly to tell Zhao Qinghe and guess what? I didn't get any more letters. He was just like that – a bit odd – and there was nothing I could do about it. I finished the first year and went home for the summer. I went to see him specially. He was buried in work. The university entrance exams were approaching. I remember how he looked, leaning against his desk doing maths problems. It was really distressing. A fug of smoke billowed out from the mosquito coils on either side of him. The ceiling fan above his head spun incessantly like a big mosquito buzzing its wings. The whole room had that sharp reek of male student on the eve of the university entrance exams. It was terrifying. Truly. I hung back in the doorway in fright.

If I hadn't got into uni, would I have been the same? I thought back to last year when I was revising for the exams. Was I like that? It really disturbed me. Then I lay down on his bed and waited until he had finished the question. I didn't mention the letters and nor did he. The atmosphere was strained. It was so difficult to talk to one another. I wanted to leave, but how could I? I wanted to tell him that I had split up with that girl, but because it felt so awkward I just couldn't get it out. Then he showed me something that really surprised me, a letter from Gao Jing. I don't remember what it said exactly but the general idea was that she, Gao Jing, had really liked Zhao Qinghe all through high school. I asked him, How come? He said something I didn't quite believe. He said: 'Actually, I liked you too and since you liked me, and if it's really true, then come back tomorrow, and fuck me.' That's what he said. I didn't believe it. Do you? But at the time I pretended to. I said, 'If you say things like that, Gao Jing won't like you anymore. Think about it. There are loads of girls out there, and quite a few good ones.' He dropped his head. It was just so screwed up.

So I tried to find something funny to talk about. I told him about some stuff at college - about what happens in the sports field. Every evening after dinner there are couples walking around the running track. After so many laps they stop and snog, or sit in the middle for a grope, while the couples who still haven't done enough laps carry on circling. Then I told him that some of them just can't hold back and they start doing it right there on the sports field. Of course, this would only happen because the climate in Guangzhou is so agreeable. Girls can wear skirts all year round and in this kind of situation, skirts are really useful.

When I got to that part Zhao Qinghe couldn't help smiling. 'I'm going to get into Sun Yat-sen University,' he said. Really. That's exactly what he said. But he didn't get into that illustrious university in the city centre. He got into a new college in University Town. Not long after, he came to Sun Yat-sen Uni to see me. I took him for a meal and a stroll around the college. Then we came to the sports field. He wanted to see what I had described. He was really excited about it. But unfortunately there wasn't anything to see. I remember I spent a lot of money taking him to a bar near the university to make him feel better.

The bar was on the edge of the slums. You know what those places are like. You've seen them. The people there are the poorest in the world and are desperate to strike it rich. They flood into Guangzhou, the city of money and opportunity, like lusty sailors full of entrepreneurial spirit. Yes, early on in their careers they stand there looking at the self-help books: the autobiographies of successful people, the tactics of how to get on in society, the secrets of how to become rich. Though these books promise to uncover the secret shortcuts to success, they emphasise the importance of getting the timing right and having the courage to persevere. The road to success is not necessarily going to be plain sailing; there's always the possibility of setbacks.

Anyhow, before getting rich and successful you will always be bored and lonely and will need some cheap and effective way to amuse yourself. The bars you find at the edge of the slums are just the best, cheap and buzzing. We came across a group of foreigners in the bar. A friend of mine was already sitting with them so Zhao Qinghe and I went over to join them.

There were several black people in the group. Most of them had come from Africa. Some might well have been the sons of chieftains. Most, to me, looked like international playboys. Whatever their status in life, their residence permits had long since run out. They were illegal aliens in China and could only come out under cover of the night. You know the analogy in the Western Han Tales about the scholar who thinks he can merge into his surroundings, like a preying mantis, simply by holding up a leaf? Good. Well, enough said.

One guy, who could have been President Obama's son and who spoke Mandarin with a slight Hunanese accent, said to me, 'Guangzhou feels like part of Africa.' This put us at our ease. But the congenial mood was short lived. Moments later Zhao Qinghe managed to completely ruin it. This is what happened. In the midst of this group of Africans was a white person who professed to be an American. This was before Obama had been elected and Bush had just decided to get bloody revenge by destroying Saddam Hussein. It was a major international event, something that we couldn't avoid talking about. The American and the Africans weren't particularly interested, but we Chinese were somehow obliged to discuss it with them as a matter of national pride.

All of a sudden we heard an insistent voice interrogating the American:

'But what about the Red Indians?'

'What about the Red Indians, then?'

'What about the Red Indians?'

Of course it had to be Zhao Qinghe. And then, as if he was practicing his English for his fourth grade diploma, he volunteered a rough translation of this interrogative sentence:

'Are there even any Red Indians left in your country?'

'Are there even any Red Indians left in your country?'

'Are there even any Red Indians left in your country?'

Li Ruiqiang is someone I've got to know quite recently. We also met in a bar. There was a third-rate rock band playing at the time. I had been dragged in to listen by a group of friends and decided it wasn't too intense. I couldn't do anything about my ears, but my eyes were looking all over. I reckoned that the bar would be the kind of place to find a girl for a one-night stand. At the time, Li Ruiqiang was also there taking a good look round. He was on his own, and looked a bit lonely. Well, neither of us found the right kind of free and easy female art student of our imaginations. He asked me for a cigarette. I gave him one and then passed him the lighter. And since that moment this one kuai lighter that I had used for about three months was lost to me forever. Afterwards, when we went looking for somewhere to have a drink, I bought another lighter. I've never mentioned it to Li Ruiqiang. Why should I? After the show it seemed only natural to find somewhere to eat raw oysters and drink beer together.

He told me about Zhao Qinghe while we were sitting at that table. I remember the plastic membrane of the disposable tablecloth fluttering in the constant flow of air from the electric fan, making me think, for a while, that there might be a typhoon coming.

'It's a real pity,' he said, 'Don't take it the wrong way. I had a friend who I think you'd get on with. His name was Zhao Qinghe. I'd really like to introduce you, but the trouble is, last year he got into a fight and was beaten to death.'

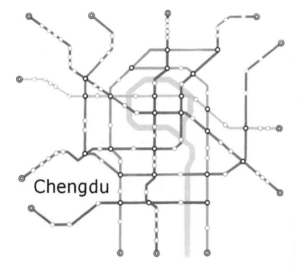
Chengdu

Kangkang's Gonna Kill That Fucker Zhao Yilu

JIE CHEN

TRANSLATED BY JOSH STENBERG

WHEN I GOT Kangkang's call it was already five, and she wanted me to be at her place by six. My plan had been to go back to my mum and dad's, but Kangkang insisted that I go to her place. When I tried to put her off, she said that she was going out at six to kill That Fucker Zhao Yilu. She was very calm, and sounded quite firm and determined. She hung up right after she was done talking. And then my battery died right after her call. I didn't have a landline in yet. I'd been waiting for the telecom bureau to offer free instalment, and this month they finally had. The ad said that they'd install the landline for free, plus give you 200 kuai in minutes. I had just put in for it two days before. But right then, all of this meant I had no way of reaching Kangkang, and I had no choice but to rush over to her place.

Whether or not That Fucker Zhao Yilu deserved to be killed – that wasn't the main thing. Whether or not Kangkang was really going to kill That Fucker Zhao Yilu – that wasn't the main thing either. The main thing was to get to Kangkang's by six. Otherwise, twenty years of friendship was going to go down the drain. I understood what the point of calling me was. I was being summoned to restrain her.

So my intention was to go over to Kangkang's and restrain her from acting on impulse. Then, when we had carefully planned it all, I would encourage her to kill That Fucker Zhao Yilu.

That Fucker Zhao Yilu was Kangkang's husband. His real name was Zhao Yilu, but not long after he married Kangkang his name became That Fucker Zhao Yilu. Kangkang had been telling the tale for a long time and in great detail, and it was perfectly clear to me how the individual in question had gone from being Darling Zhao Yilu to being just Zhao Yilu and then finally That Fucker Zhao Yilu. Although on many subjects my opinion is diametrically opposed to Kangkang's, I never try to divert Kangkang's train of thought into what I think is the right direction. It's not worth trying. Me and Kangkang have been friends for twenty years, and I am wholly aware of what a waste of time and effort it is to try and get Kangkang to start thinking straight. And I'm not the kind of person to waste time and effort.

According to Kangkang, That Fucker Zhao Yilu had taken 10,000 kuai of their money and given it to some girlfriend of his. What can you do with a man like that, besides kill him?

It was my opinion that she should poison him rather than just butcher him. I mean, the knife wasn't a good idea; poison was the thing, like in that old story where Golden Lotus kills her ugly dwarf of a husband. My idea would have done a lot to help Kangkang liberate herself from all those feelings of hate. I know Kangkang like the back of my hand. What counts for her is the idea of it all. She's not big on the action itself.

I left home at 5:20. I washed my face with a cleanser, and then put on moisturiser and liquid foundation even though it was still uneven on my nose. My nose has the texture of orange peel, and unless I spend twenty or thirty minutes putting foundation on, it looks awful. But, for Kangkang's sake, I had to risk it. My hair was all messy and so I gelled it down. I put lip-liner and eye-liner on, and then I didn't even do my eyebrows, skipping instead straight to the lipstick. There just wasn't time. I had to get to Kangkang's and stop her from leaving home with a concealed vegetable knife. I didn't know where she would be heading to kill her husband, though I did know that he hadn't been living there for a few days. The main thing was to put a stop to the vegetable knife. Kangkang just doesn't have any style, she would totally take the vegetable knife. You might as well use a watermelon knife, aesthetically speaking. That ditz just hasn't got a clue.

The other day I was at her place and killed two cockroaches with her watermelon knife, and then I put the knife on the top shelf of her cupboard. The thing about cockroaches and the watermelon knife is sort of a special trick I know. Most people can't get the hang of it. If Kangkang wanted to kill him with the watermelon knife, she wouldn't be able to find it, because I forgot to tell her where I put it. Actually, when the murderer's a woman, the whole thing will sound much better if she uses a dagger. A woman's soft white hand slipping the dagger from her pocket, the cold blade gleaming, setting off her red lips, her ivory teeth...now that would be aesthetically satisfying. On the other hand, there's probably not much chance of getting your hands on a dagger. Weapons like that are subject to restrictions; I don't know where you would go to buy something like that.

At 5:25 I reached the gate of the housing estate where I live, but then I remembered my apartment door. Had I locked it? I had no memory of even touching the lock. I stood struggling with my doubts at the gate for two minutes and then decided I had to go back and see. Of course, it's not fun and games if Kangkang is committing a murder, but on the other hand she hadn't committed it yet, and nobody could say whether she was really going to or not, and moreover, maybe That Fucker Zhao Yilu would be really hard to kill, maybe as soon as she got near him Zhao Yilu would just tackle her, that was entirely possible. But if I had really forgotten to lock the door, that would be a disaster. Suppose my place had been ransacked by the time I got back from Kangkang's! The worst thing was, I had just taken 3,000 kuai in cash out of the bank and put it in my bedside drawer, to give it to my parents that night. My parents are renovating, so I figure it's the least a good daughter could do. My brother put up most of the money, 30,000 kuai. He's loaded.

I sprinted back to the eleventh apartment of the seventh floor of the fourth building of the housing estate, and was out of breath by the time I got there. I don't mean that I was *panting* for breath, I mean that I was just clean out of it. With my exhausted arms I tugged at the door, and with exhausted feet, I kicked at it, thus proving to myself that it was locked. Then, I leaned against the hallway wall for three minutes. Actually, I really wanted to sit down in the stairwell, but the stairwell was totally filthy. I don't know what we pay a maintenance fee for. You can lean on the walls, because they used latex instead of ordinary paint, which is pretty much the only nice thing about this apartment. Can you believe it's 3,600 kuai per square meter?

When I got my breath back a little, I started sprinting across the estate again. Luckily, I had had the foresight to select the short brown wedge-heel ankle boots. In point of fact, given the length and colour of the little black thin-wool twill suit pants I was wearing, my black high-heel ankle boots would have been a better choice. But, since Kangkang was going to kill someone, did it really matter if my boots and pants weren't perfectly coordinated? I'm a very clear-headed person, and when it comes to helping friends, I always keep my priorities straight.

At exactly 5:35, I passed through the estate gates. My watch is very accurate, it's just an ordinary Tianba, but very accurate. My colleague A Fish Called Wanda just bought an Omega, and so what? It's not as accurate as my Tianba. When A Fish Called Wanda was showing off her Omega, she looked exactly like the woman with the face like a knife in the British movie A Fish Called Wanda. The name really suits her. I've job-hopped four times, this is already my fifth company, and you wouldn't believe it, but every time I start a new job there's someone from a movie in it, large as life. There was Dumb and Dumber and The Little Mole Qiuqiu and Who's

Your Daddy and the Magnificent White Bone Spirit and then
A Fish Called Wanda.

I hurried toward Kangkang's place. I was on foot, not in a car
or bus or anything. I live near Shuinian River and Kangkang's
place is on Yushuang Road. If I hailed a cab, it would have
been at least 5 kuai 40, which is the minimum fare. If I'd taken
one of those pedicabs it would have been at least 5 kuai too.
If I'd taken a motorbike sidecar it would have been a little
cheaper, probably only 3 kuai, but last month I took one of
those and I had a fall. We were going along and the axle broke,
but luckily I have quick reflexes and escaped without injury.
Thinking about money matters is so annoying. Biking it
would only have been ten minutes. Except, I don't know how
to ride a bike. This little shortcoming of mine makes my life
a lot more complicated, and I end up spending 200 kuai more
on transport than A Fish Called Wanda and all that lot. Usually
they bike to work, and only take a cab if the weather's crap,
like it's really windy or raining or whatever. The payment on
my apartment is 2400 kuai a month. Kangkang's got it made.
It takes her five minutes to walk to work, and her dad's an
official and connived some way to get her that apartment,
although actually her salary's about the same as mine. And that
little snake always makes me pay half the bill when we go out,
with no ifs, ands or buts.

Still, walking briskly, it wouldn't take more than twenty
minutes. When I say walk briskly, I mean: walk two steps, run
two steps. That would get me to Kangkang's by 5:55, although
I would still have to climb up to the third floor. Which meant
I would definitely be knocking on Kangkang's door by 5:58.

By 5:47, I was already at the Yushuang Road intersection,
which was two minutes earlier than planned. I halted,
intending to rest for a couple of minutes. Sweat was dripping
off my back.

Wait, did I lock the door? I locked it, didn't I? But when
I went back to look this time, might I have unlocked it? Then

did I relock it after?

Damn it all to hell. I can't run back from here.

Que Será Será.

A chubby woman walked up to me from the side and patted me on the shoulder. She came up to me from the side, not from behind, so I saw her out of the corner of my eye. I don't like it when strangers pat me on the shoulder, so I turned to look at her and frowned.

She smiled and came even closer, 'Lady, you need some receipts?'

'No.'

'Need a diploma?'

'No.'

'You need an official stamp?'

Hell, the woman could do it all. I looked her right in the eyes and said, 'No.'

'Well, how about a dagger?'

Wow! A dagger! I looked carefully at this woman who sold receipts and diplomas and official stamps and daggers, and though she was a little chubby, she was actually quite beautiful, with impeccable teeth. With intelligence she interpreted my expression and immediately said, 'My shop's right here, come take a look.' She indicated a little storefront no more than four or five meters away. It was a sex shop. I went in, a little astonished that she had been able to tell that a woman who had just been standing, resting, for a couple of minutes, would be someone who needed to buy a receipt, diploma, stamp or dagger. Was it written on my forehead?

The chubby woman fished through a big pile of condom cartons and took out a large paper box from underneath. It opened to reveal five or six little knives. Ah, daggers; daggers just right for concealment. Not bad at all – filigree silver knife handles, inset with turquoise. I took one that had three turquoise stones surrounding a piece of red coral: very beautiful. Was it really made of silver, turquoise and red coral? Who cared if it was real; in any case it was beautiful. I picked up the one I had chosen and raised it slowly up to the corner of the chubby woman's mouth, while she smiled cooperatively – yes indeed, the cold gleaming blade, red lips, her ivory teeth! Spectacular!

I didn't haggle, and just gave her 80 kuai. She said there was no sheath and no box, so she wrapped it in a fresh paper towel and handed it to me. I put the knife carefully at the bottom of my bag, thought for a moment and said, 'Two for one. Throw in some of these Durex condoms.' And I grabbed a box of 20 condoms, but the chubby woman snatched it away and gave me one with only two instead.

I looked at my watch. Forget it, I'm not going to bicker about it. No time for that.

As I ran, I looked at my watch. 5:55. A little behind schedule. There were lots of public telephones in the little dry goods stores that lined the road, but it made no sense to stop and call rather than to just keep running. No matter what, running it would take me at least 5 minutes. I was really out of breath. That little snake Kangkang was really doing a number on me.

There was construction on Yushuang Road, and the whole place was dug up, with stones and mud everywhere you looked. My boots! I had only bought them a month before – they're Le Saundas. Even on sale they cost me 360.

Six o'clock on the dot. I still had at least two minutes before I would reach Kangkang's. And that was without counting the stairs. I was hoping that Kangkang wouldn't leave the house on time. But that little snake has plenty of shortcomings and only one redeeming feature: punctuality. A woman needs a lot of qualities; like for instance not howling about how she's going to kill her husband, because if you're going to kill him you might as well shut up and get on with it; or like for instance not doing something as tacky as pocketing a vegetable knife and heading out the door; like for instance improving her aesthetic sensibility. Like for instance knowing a thing or two about how to get somebody to throw in a freebee when you make a purchase. Like also for instance, how That Fucker Zhao Yilu fancied me first and then when he saw Kangkang set his sights on her instead, and how I didn't take it to heart. I was even maid of honour. Also for instance like how although it still gave me a little pang every time I saw That Fucker Zhao Yilu, I didn't let it affect our friendship. And also like how even though last time That Fucker Zhao Yilu pretended to accidentally touch my hand when Kangkang was in the kitchen getting water, I just instantly slid a little further away. At the time, I was all flustered, but in my mind I sternly denounced his fickle behaviour. And also like how, even though I can't really have feelings for any other guy because of the shadow Zhao Yilu casts on my emotions, in my heart I still haven't let the hope of a wonderful life, a wonderful marriage, die out…

I ran like the wind. Why was it that I wanted so much to put that dagger to good use? Why did I want that so, so much?

By the time I was downstairs outside of Kangkang's building it was 6:02. With nothing left but my loyal and steadfast heart and my spirit of self-sacrifice, I basically had to crawl up to the third floor and throw myself at the buzzer.

The door opened and – That Fucker Zhao Yilu appeared!

He was at home. What about Kangkang? If That Fucker Zhao Yilu was at home, who was Kangkang setting off to murder?

'Is….Kang…kang…home?' I managed to pant out.

'She went out, she'll be back soon.' That Fucker Zhao Yilu said. 'Come in.'

I stood there and didn't move a muscle.

'Didn't you move out?'

'We patched it up. Just now.'

'You patched it up, just like that? Just right now?'

'Hey, she had it all wrong. I just had to explain it all. It was a big fight about nothing. Come in.'

Why should That Fucker Zhao Yilu be at home? Had Kangkang changed her plan of action after she phoned me, and decided to lure him home and kill him there? Wasn't it all over between the two of them? So how come he could just show up like that? Could it be that Kangkang had used some trick of hers, who knows what kind of trick exactly, but some trick between the two of them, and lured him over? And after Zhao Yilu had come, he had astutely perceived her plot and with decisive nimble strokes resolved the crisis – which is to say, he had used Kangkang's own vegetable knife to 'resolve' her, just like in that old movie *The Sea Wolves* where Roger Moore twists the wrist of the female agent so that instead of stabbing him with the dagger she gets stabbed with it herself? I always said a dagger was what was needed, not a vegetable knife. With a vegetable knife you can only hack, not stab. Had Kangkang been hacked to death? Had he just committed the deed and been about to make his escape when I rang the buzzer and ran smack into him?

Abruptly, I took a big step backwards. The fear made my body alive in every fibre. I rushed down the stairs and smashed right into someone. It was Kangkang. Kangkang alive and in the flesh, looking like a steamed bun, her chubby cheeks rosy, beaming like she had just found a wallet lying on the ground.

The impact knocked the two plastic bags out of her hand. A few takeaway containers lay face-down on the ground, steaming, while apples and oranges rolled down the stairs and a bottle of red wine lay smashed on the floor.

Kangkang didn't have time to wipe the grin off her face, so with her astonishment wreathed in smiles, she looked at the things on the ground, and then looked at the bag I had let fall to the ground. I looked at it too. None of the other items in

my bag had fallen out, my keys and address book and mobile
had all stayed inside, the only things that had fallen out were
the package of Durexes and a dagger freed from its paper
towel, its blade coldly gleaming...

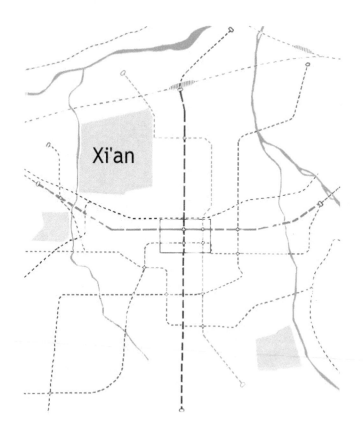

Rendezvous at the Castle Hotel

YI SHA

TRANSLATED BY YU YAN CHEN

CHOU GUANG, A self-funded student from Zhongshan City of Guangdong, stopped me at the entrance to my office. He had come at the right time as I only show my face there briefly, once a day. Our impromptu meeting occurred at around ten o'clock, between the first and the last two lecture slots of the morning. After a brief greeting, he introduced himself as someone who 'writes poetry', and asked me what other poets I hang out with in Xi'an. I told him frankly that those I was in regular contact with were Shen Qi, Nan Mo, and the husband and wife team of Li Zhen and Liu Yali. This was ten years back; Qin Bazi had not moved to Xi'an at that point, so I did not know him then. When we became friends later, he said that I was too honest with literary youths: 'Sometimes, one doesn't need to be so honest.' But my position has always been consistent: Who *hasn't* started out as a literary youth, and haven't we all hoped to bump into good people and welcoming faces? But what was said later that morning made me determined not to talk to Chou Guang any further.

'Are you guys in a group?' he asked, but the tone of his Cantonese-accented Mandarin made it sound like an interrogation.

'We are not a group; we just meet up from time to time to talk about poetry,' I replied rather formally.

45

'Oh, so you only get together to write and talk about poetry?'

'Yes. What about it?'

'This poetry business is trivial, no matter how grand it might sound.'

'Excuse me, I've got to go to my class.'

In reality, I wasn't scheduled to lead the last two lectures that morning, yet I sensed that it was time to terminate the conversation. After a quick goodbye, I went back to the halls. I thought about the incident and the person I had just met, even took into consideration his hometown, which was also the hometown of Sun Yat-sen.[2] Since he considered poetry trivial, he must have come here to belong to a scene, but what kind of scene was he after? What did he really want? On second thoughts, who gives a damn what he wanted to do? I had no desire to see that person ever again.

I stayed in the halls till midday, reading and writing a couple of poems as and when I felt inspired. That was my daily routine ten years ago. At 11:30, when the student broadcast started playing over the loud speaker, I would be holding my lunch box, setting out to dine at the canteen for teachers and employees. But that day a knock sounded at the door. It was a casual yet heavy knock, the kind an acquaintance would deliver. But when I opened the door, I saw Chou Guang instead.

---

2. Sun Yat-sen (12 November 1866 – 12 March 1925) was a revolutionary, who played an instrumental role in the overthrow of the Qing dynasty during the Xinhai Revolution. He then became the first provisional president when the Republic of China was founded in 1912. Sun is referred to as the "Father of the Nation" in the Republic of China, and the "forerunner of democratic revolution" in the People's Republic of China. There are many variations to his name, but two of the most frequently used are Sun Wen (his original name) and Sun Zhongshan.

'Let's go eat. I've already made a reservation at the hotpot[3] restaurant near the university gates.' As Chou Guang spoke those words standing in the hallway, his expression, tone of voice, and hand gestures all made him look as if he were an acquaintance of mine.

The invitation seemed impossible to decline. So I said, 'Let's go then.'

When we arrived, the female owner greeted us amiably. There weren't lots of customers then, but Chou Guang had booked ahead all the same.

We chatted as we ate. I asked about his hometown because of the Sun Wen connection. Chou Guang was indeed an amazing fellow; everything he said was absolute bullshit. I had recently seen a film entitled *Sun Zhongshan*, directed by Ding Yinnan. The cinematographer was Hou Yong, another Xi'an native. This film had an intense descriptive style, and I suddenly couldn't get a certain image out of my mind: an enormous table occupies the frame; Sun Wen is bending over while holding onto a corner of it with his big hands, as more and more silver coins drop down from the sky, hitting the table with splashing sounds. The film was about Sun Wen's revolution and how it sprang from overseas donations, a resilient movement undeterred by many setbacks. Eight years later I happened to be driving through Zhujiang Triangle with my editor from the magazine I was moonlighting at. That was my first trip to Guangdong and on the way from Shenzhen to Guangzhou, we stopped by Cuiheng Village in Zhongshan to pay our respects to Dr. Sun Yat-sen. We did not visit the centre of Zhongshan City, and even if we had, I would not have remembered to contact Chou Guang, the self-funded student from the hometown of Sun Zhongshan. Besides, by that point we had long since lost touch.

---

3. A type of Chinese cuisine in which side dishes of raw food are given to customers to be cooked in a boiling pot of broth.

During our meal, Chou Guang divulged his backstory. His family was wealthy (a typical characteristic of students from Guangdong). His father operated a supermarket in Zhongshan City. Since he had been unable to get into university after graduating from high school, he helped his father manage the supermarket. There were many tourists who came to visit Zhongshan (paying tribute to Sun Zhongshan, of course), so business at the supermarket flourished. Then one day his father had a sudden revelation and said to him: 'Guangzai,' he said, 'go find a place and learn some foreign languages. More and more foreigners come to the shop each day. If neither of us knows any other language, it will have a negative impact on business.' As for the overseas tourists flocking to Zhongshan, besides those coming from Hong Kong and Taiwan, the next on the list was Japan, so Chou Guang chose to study Japanese. As to why he picked Xi'an, his reply both surprised and embarrassed me. He said that I was in Xi'an and he came here for me. He said, 'What damn Japanese am I going to learn?' He came to Xi'an to write poetry. He had been writing poetry since middle school. He'd first read my poems in the *Youth Poetry Magazine* but had no idea I was teaching on the campus until he sat next to a girl last night at a seminar, who happened to be one of my students. That was why he came looking for me this morning.

Putting it like that made me feel as if I was somehow responsible for him, and that was why I decided to show him around.

At some point during the meal, I lit a cigarette and asked him what was the 'group' he was referring to, and why he had asked me about it. Of course I said it with a grin.

He smiled too and said, 'Don't get me wrong.' He said he detected a revolutionary passion in my poems, and he imagined that I was surrounded by a group of kindred spirits.

I said, 'Don't scare me. I only write some poems! As you

say, it's trivial.'

He said poetry needs revolution and literature needs revolution. There should be a renaissance in China.

'Could you tell me then: who exactly are we up against in this revolution?'

'Those old fellows.'

'Which old fellows?'

'I don't know either.'

'Then let's make sure we know who we are revolting against first.'

I discovered that he knew very little about literature or the literary scene; and random as it might be, time slipped through our fingers as we chatted. Before I knew it, it was already 2:30 in the afternoon.

It was my younger sister (I sometimes need to remind myself she's biologically related to me) who pointed out that Chou Guang is very handsome. The similarity between Chou Guang and my sister is that both failed their university entrance exams. After her high school graduation (she took the entrance exam twice), she too became a self-funded foreign language student on campus. However, she was in a different class because she studied English. One day she casually dropped him into conversation:'Who is that handsome guy who comes to visit you in your office so often?'

'Is he handsome?' I asked, 'Why have I never noticed?' My sister said it was because I am a guy. Not only did she think that Chou Guang was handsome, but he had become the topic of discussion among girls in classrooms full of self-funded students.

I said,'Really? I think he isn't that much more handsome than I am. Why don't I get this kind of attention?' She said it is mainly because he looks more southern, like someone from Hong Kong or Taiwan. It was a more popular look. What my sister said shut me up. Yet her final remark about Chou Guang left a deep impression on me because it subsequently proved to be true. He was too aware of his own good looks and that made him unattractive, she explained; only the boys who didn't know it were truly adorable.

One day Chou Guang came to my place while I was shaving. He picked up a small mirror I placed on the table and looked at his own reflection. He praised himself while playing with his hair: 'How handsome! What the heck do I need to write poetry for when I am so handsome? Damn! That's what a woman would do!' While I was busy getting goosebumps at this I heard his question: 'Poetry Brother' (he insisted on calling me that ever since we met), 'do you think I look more like Leslie Cheung or Andy Lau? Half of the girls in my class say I look like Leslie Cheung and the other half say I look like Andy Lau. But I feel I look more like Chow Yun-Fat. What do you think?'

I replied while shaving that he didn't look like any of them. There was one who really looked like him though. He earnestly asked who. I said, 'Eric Tsang.'

He started to whine at once: 'Poetry Brother, are you kidding me? I can't be that ugly.' Then I said he looked like Joey Wong. 'But that's a woman,' he said.

By then I had finished shaving: 'You think you are not a woman?!'

After all, this chap was slightly troubled; a man of little substance who wanted nothing more than to keep up appearances. I could understand and forgive why he revealed himself so completely on that occasion. On the one hand, he was a nobody to us. He assembled his poems into a pamphlet and distributed it everywhere, but this was only met with deafening silence from key critics like Shen Qi and Li Zhen. My opinion was that he lacked something fundamental when it came to writing poetry, but I did not dare mention that to his face. The poems he sent to all those literary magazines (whose addresses had been provided by me) were like cows made of mud thrown into the ocean. And yet, with the ladies, he was a knight in shining armour, a prince with boundless popularity. On two occasions, he complained to me with a frown: he had been troubled by love (his own words) everyday because there were too many girls pursuing him, and he had no idea which one to choose. I said, 'Why don't you bring all of those girls to me? I will solve the problem for you. After all I'm not busy and what a way to pass the time!' He shook his head painfully. Anyhow, he was searching for balance, compensating for the void in one part of his personality with the psychological advantage he boasted in the other. The emptier he felt at one end, the more he needed to emphasise or exaggerate this psychological advantage at the other. This made him even more troubled as a result.

In the literary circles of Xi'an, Ms L was a well-known character. She neither wrote nor painted but was famous nonetheless, or should I say 'infamous', as the 'Mistress of the Masters.' Legend has it that she successively (other versions say 'simultaneously') hooked up with famous writer So-and-so, famous painter and calligrapher So-and-so, as well as emerging young writer So-and-so. The first two were already 'masters' in the Chinese sense, and the third was rising in popularity. The rumour mill grinded out something even more fascinating: apparently, all three of them were nobodies before they met her, and only once she got her hands on them did they suddenly attain the unlikely heights of their current success. I had heard about her when I was attending college in Beijing. When I first returned to Xi'an for work, one poet from Shanghai even wrote to me saying, 'All she needs now is to create a poet; you should pull your finger out!' Of course I refrained from looking up this Ms L, who had the power to turn stones into gold. Do I look crazy? But one day I received a letter from her, saying she read several of my poems in *One Line Magazine*, edited by Yan Li in New York. She said she could see potential in them and hoped that I would stop by her house for a visit.

I went to Ms L's house with Chou Guang around dusk. After dinner, we rode our bikes to the eastern suburb. I was not simply being presumptuous bringing Chou Guang along with me. He happened to be there when I received the letter and he insisted on coming along. His understanding of the rumours and legends that surrounded the literary scene had far exceeded his understanding of poetry, and naturally he wanted to meet this legendary Ms L. That day he had dressed especially smart and his hair shone damply with excessive mousse, as if he had just trudged through a rainstorm. The collar of his shirt (fresh on, of course) was snow white, and contrasted with his brown skin tone typical of the Guangdong region. I cracked a joke: 'You look as if you're going on a blind date.' He replied that he had a feeling Ms L was about to fall in love with him. He said that the three she had been with could form an ugly men's club (a conclusion he made after seeing their photos in the press). I smiled on my bike in the deepening dusk. It was then that I began to take a genuine interest in the meeting – because this silly fellow was tacking along!

The idiom 'beauty beyond her prime' didn't quite apply to Ms L. It was true that she was no longer young – she was clearly into her 40s – but she wasn't necessarily a 'beauty' either. I think even in her prime, she couldn't have been that attractive. There was no one else at home that day but us. Legend had it she had been through a marriage a long time ago. After we both sat down, she made us two cups of coffee. I asked if I could smoke, she replied, 'Of course,' and the ashtray she brought out looked like a piece of art. Anyhow, we were in a sophisticated environment. Although the hostess was neither pretty nor young, she enlightened us with more than enough elegance and grace in this backwater city of Xi'an. The memories associated with that conversation are blurry now. I only recall that she mentioned lots of famous names, as if there was no-one she didn't know in the literary world. What gave me a slight thrill was that someone (a celebrity) had mentioned my name in a letter to her. At least two of the names she mentioned were serious heavyweights, and I only realised it later, so I respected her somewhat for that. Those two names she mentioned were Japanese, as she had just returned from Japan where she met them – 'phenomenal writers' she called them. One of them was Oe Kenzaburo. Oe received the Nobel Prize four years later. The other was Tanikawa Shuntarou – the best poet in Japan and one of my favourites. I was already fond of his poetry when I was still an undergraduate, but somehow I'd forgotten his name over the years. The conversation hardly touched upon anything pertaining to literature itself, but I had nothing against someone like Ms L. She could create a certain atmosphere and occasionally even make things happen. She was the type of person we might call a 'literary activist', but she was not doing these things on behalf of any organisation.

Throughout the night, Chou Guang barely contributed to the conversation. He was unable to chime in. There were two occasions when I tried to steer the conversation towards him. I said, 'This is a young poet full of potential,' but our hostess paid no attention and continued to dominate proceedings. When you ignore Chou Guang, he tends to get back at you with a nit-picking look. He wore that same pathetic expression almost all evening.

It seemed that the old whore had nothing substantial to offer him other than a few famous names. Sometime after ten, as soon as we'd descended her stairs, and before we'd even left the corridor, Chou Guang started to curse. 'Who's going to want that old turd? I wouldn't have her even if she chased after me.' He was still upset as we rode our bikes onto the main road. 'Poetry Brother, I am not having a go, but why did you put up with that old whore! I wish I could have got up and left…'

I really did not expect this kid to be mired in such nonsense. I suddenly twisted my handlebars and blocked his way, which took him by surprise: 'Are you done with this bullshit? Listen, in the future, don't follow me wherever I go.'

As for our rendezvous at the Castle Hotel, what this actually entailed was firstly booking the rooms at the hotel and then fetching the guests from the airport. I remember the date of the rendezvous very clearly. It all happened around 8pm on 11 May 1991, because 30 April was my wedding day. I had taken ten days' holiday for the wedding and returned to work on the morning of the 11th (I had two classes). In my office that morning, I received a long distance call from Taiwan. I quickly became busy organising the pick-up for later that afternoon. The call came from the Taiwan poet, Yang Ping. I met him when I was at college in Beijing, and we'd corresponded ever since. Yang Ping had asked me to host four reverent poets from Taiwan. They were Guan Guan, Zhang Mo, Bi Guo and Da Huang, colleagues of his from the famous poetry magazine *Genesis*. I was supposed to arrange for a hotel, and secure a car for sightseeing (the cost of which was to be covered by them). The task didn't seem that difficult, and I immediately thought of someone who was capable of helping. I was right. I rang Ms L immediately after I received Yang Ping's call. As expected, she was very friendly, saying, 'Let them stay at the Castle Hotel, it's four-star!' She knew someone there and could get a 50% discount. As for the vehicle, she said she could find one from a government work unit through her connections, that way the driver could get some extra cash on the side. They would be more than willing to do it anyway, and the price could be negotiated face to face. The four reverent gentlemen were already in China by then. They had visited Chengde on the 1st of May, then went back to Beijing, as they were due to fly out that evening. I asked over the phone whether Ms L would like us to prepare a sign with their names; she requested one and said that her driver would handle it.

That was how it went. Ms L, the driver and I met up that evening at the lobby of Castle Hotel at 7pm. While we were booking rooms at the front desk someone unexpected arrived – Chou Guang. I had no idea how he got there or how he had learned about the meeting. My gut feeling indicated that it had to be through Ms L – it couldn't be anyone else. I didn't bother greeting him and tried to act as if he didn't exist. The booking process was simple as there was more to be done when the guests actually arrived. Since the flight was due in at some time after nine o'clock, and the airport (still the good old airport!) was nearby, Ms L suggested that we hang out at the cafe until it was time to leave. She said not to rush over there – how could an airport be more comfortable than this place? We were about to head over to the cafe, when one of Ms L's acquaintances appeared; a rather pretty young woman who happened to be the manager of the hotel's karaoke bar. She addressed Ms L constantly as 'Big Sister', saying, 'Why do you want to go to the café? Why don't you sing karaoke and enjoy some coffee at my place? You can even dance if you want to!' That was how we found ourselves going up to the bar on the third floor, and staying there until past eight o'clock, before eventually getting up to leave. But there was a problem; Chou Guang was nowhere to be found. There was no trace of him anywhere in the bar. We couldn't find him at the lobby either. I said, 'Let's not look for him anymore, he wasn't supposed to come anyway.' I asked Ms L on our way to the airport how Chou Guang had learned about the pick-up. Ms L replied that she happened to receive a call from him after talking to me on the phone at noon. He asked her what I had been doing lately and she mentioned the pick-up tonight; that was why he came. 'What happened?' she asked, 'You guys have an argument?'

I said, 'No, it was just that we haven't seen much of each other.'

'He must have had an emergency,' she said. 'Perhaps he'll be waiting for us in the lobby after we pick these people up.

The boy has that kind of style.'

The pick-up went smoothly. The four men were lots of fun: they were young at heart indeed. We returned to the Castle Hotel and stayed in their rooms for about half an hour, but Chou Guang never showed up again, and that was the last I saw of him for nine years, until a few days ago.

I was in my office and my pager just started buzzing. Two lines appeared: *Poetry Brother, Chou Guang is waiting for you at Room 1357 at the Castle Hotel. Please come.* In recent years, various people have suddenly begun to resurface in my life. Regardless of their social standing, they all still want to meet up and have a drink whenever they arrive in Xi'an. I can't complain, given that they're so enthusiastic. So I usually just grab my wallet and hop in a taxi. This was no exception, as any slight feeling of discomfort towards him had long since faded away.

I never expected the miniature Yeltsin standing in Room 1357 of the Castle to be the same handsome lad of years before, however. I burst into a raucous laughter: 'You look like neither Leslie Cheung nor Andy Lau, definitely not Chow Yun-Fat! You've returned to Mainland China and transformed into a Liu Huang!'

'A shame I didn't get to grow anything these years, other than this waistline,' he said, as he let me in.

I asked him: 'You must be rich now, right?'

He said, 'Go figure, we only had one supermarket nine years ago, now we have four of them. It is not difficult for Cantonese people to make money.' His Mandarin had greatly deteriorated, and along with the drastic change in his appearance, I simply couldn't believe that the person in front of me wasn't someone else.

He insisted on treating me at the Castle and declined my invitation to savour the famous kebabs of Xi'an's Muslim Quarter. I told him this place could burn a hole in his pocket. He replied, 'No big deal.' He said another reason he wanted to dine at the hotel was because he wanted to tell me something over dinner regarding an event that occurred at the hotel years before.

The following is the gist of the conversation between Chou Guang and I as we dined at the Chinese restaurant on the second floor of the Castle Hotel. There was no tape recording, but it was recorded in my head:

'Poetry Brother, do you know why I disappeared from the karaoke bar upstairs that night, the night we picked up those Taiwanese poets? Do you know where I went?'

'How would I know? I was surprised when you suddenly appeared that day. I finally understood after I asked Ms L on our way to the airport.'

'What do you remember about the karaoke bar that night?'

'Not much. There weren't that many customers that day, I remember that.'

'Exactly. It was a bit early, not even eight o'clock. Most of the customers hadn't finished their meals; most of them were probably down here in the restaurant.'

'All of us seemed to be sitting at the same table that evening.'

'Exactly, you, me, Ms L and the driver.'

'That pretty young manager greeted us, gave everyone a cup of coffee and encouraged us to select the songs for the karaoke bar.'

'Ms L picked out 'Salute to the Heroes', a song from the movie *Heroic Sons and Daughters* that played at the same time, in which Wang Cheng[4] sacrificed his life. She performed the song with such a screeching voice I found it hilarious.'

'I saw you laughing in the dark, and I felt that you were insincere towards Ms L.'

'What are you talking about?'

---

4. A fictional character in the patriotic 1964 film. A soldier in the Chinese Volunteer Army during the Korean War, Wang Cheng heroically defends a command point on a hill after his entire unit is wiped out. His line 'Fire at me!' became a national catchphrase.

'Do you remember what you sang?'

"Just like your tenderness".'

'That's right. You have an excellent memory.'

'That was my first karaoke.'

'You sang well but the voice faded slightly when you got to a high note. Do you remember what I sang?'

'No, I don't.'

'You were too busy chatting with Ms L. You were constantly whispering to each other that night.'

'Her understanding of the Taiwanese poetry scene was limited to Yu Kwang-Chung and Zheng Chouyu. I told her I considered Ya Xuan and Luo Fu to be at the very top and, out of the four visitors, Guan Guan to be the best.'

'She listened to you very attentively and her expression showed her respect for you. I left at that precise moment.'

'Where did you go?'

'Nowhere in particular. I went to the bathroom once; hung out a while by the entrance of the bar. You two were still deep in conversation when I came back, while the driver sat by idly. I didn't go back to that particular table, but sat down at an empty table and ordered a beer.'

'Where did you go after that? You were not at the bar when we left some time after eight.'

'Do you remember a waiter? Very tall and thin?'

'No. Male or female?'

'Male. There weren't that many customers. He was practically the only one there.'

'I don't recall.'

'Do you know why I've brought up the events of that night?'

'I was about to ask you. You're torturing me. This is a nice meal but you are killing my appetite.'

'My apologies, please, please, please... Let's eat and chat, eat and chat.'

'Go ahead and tell me.'

'Do you still remember the murder that happened at the

Castle Hotel nine years ago?'

'Yes, I do. Two old Japanese female tourists were killed in their room after suffering from multiple knife wounds.'

'Correct. You remember this rather vividly.'

'Didn't they resolve the case already? Initially the suspect was a temporary employee who fixed showerheads for the hotel chain, but subsequently they discovered that it was a professional assassin hired by their clan. The killer also stayed at the Castle and pretended to be a tourist. It had something to do with an inheritance in their family. It seemed that one of their nephews wanted them dead. Those two old ladies were sisters, right?'

'Yes, yes, yes, you are right on the mark.'

'I am not the only one. Any ordinary Xi'an resident can tell you many details of the case.'

'But did you know that it happened on 11 May 1991, the night we picked up the Taiwanese poets?'

'No.'

'Did you know the case happened in Room 1357 where I am staying tonight?'

'No.'

'Did you know the night this happened I was *in* Room 1357 – the scene of the crime – for one and a half hours?'

'No. Don't scare me, man. I don't have the stomach for it.'

'Alright then, let's talk about it in the room after we finish our meal. It will be more authentic at the scene.'

The following is the gist of Chou Guang's description after he and I returned to Room 1357. There was no recording but it was all recorded in my head:

I asked for a beer after sitting down at an empty table behind you. The waiter brought it over first, then he came over again later. That was ten minutes after I had finished singing the second song. I had nothing to do but sing that night and I sang two songs by Wang Jie. The second time the waiter came by was to change the ashtray. After he changed it he placed a small piece of scrumpled paper in front of me in a very definite manner. I opened it up and it said, *Sir, someone is waiting for you at the lobby.* It was written using the ballpoint pen used to order songs.

I was suddenly excited to receive such a note. I had no idea who was looking for me. It didn't cross my mind how it would be possible for someone to look for me at such a place. I was excited by the mystery of it all. I immediately went to the lobby on receiving the note. Before leaving I glanced in your direction and saw that you and Ms L were still engaged in intimate conversation. I waited for about five minutes on the couch there and tried to guess who would come to seek me out from the crowd.

'Sir, how are you?' Someone appeared before me; it was the waiter, the one who had given me the note in the first place.

'Sir, I would like to talk to you about something.' He said this and sat down on the couch next to me. 'You sing well, look nice and appear very professional. Sir, you are not a client in this hotel, right? What I meant was that you're not staying here?'

'No, I only came here to hang out.'

'Sir, I have this request. If I tell you about it and if you agree, we can make a deal and there is the possibility of further collaboration in the future. But if you don't agree, you must pretend you never heard any of it. Don't tell anyone. Let's be friends.'

'Go ahead, as long as it doesn't involve drug dealing or something.'

'Don't joke around, Sir. Why would I suggest something that risked having both our heads chopped off? Let me tell you, there are these two old Japanese ladies, tourists, they have nothing to do at night and they want a young man for relaxation. The price is high, 2,000 RMB. What do you say?'

I got it. I sat there frozen for about a minute, then I

pretended to be very experienced and said, 'It's a deal.'

'Excellent!' He came closer to me and said, 'I'll call them now. Go up there after ten minutes, remember Room 1357. Come back to the club after you finish, I'll buy you a drink.'

'Will you take a cut from the 2,000?' I asked.

'No, it's all yours. I've had my tips already.' He left after that.

I began to regret my decision as those ten minutes crept by, waiting on the couch, standing in the elevator. In the end the only thing that prompted me to do it was an unshakeable trace of curiosity. You know that I never went without either women or money, right?

My knees went soft that night as I stood in front of Room 1357. After hesitating for a moment, I rang the bell and the door opened. An old lady stuck her head out. She looked like a ghost. As I entered I saw another one, just like her. They turned out to be twins. The Japanese I had studied for less than a year in this city seemed to come in handy that evening. They invited me to sit on the sofa, one of them made me a cup of tea and we talked very briefly, mostly just small talk. Then they suggested that I go for a shower. I undressed in front of them and entered the bathroom. I adjusted the water to a cooler temperature and tried to relax. When I came out of the bathroom, they had changed into pyjamas. The bedside lamp was dimmed and the room had a strong scent of perfume. I still pretended to be experienced and asked, Who goes first? Both giggled and said that they would do it together. Of course everything was said in Japanese. They asked me to lie down on the inner part of the bed and both bent down at the same time to lick at me, the way you see them do it in Japanese pornos. I hadn't watched too many of them so it all felt very novel. I gradually got into the mood, and even before they started to fight over who would blow the flute first, the flute was standing straight up on its own. All in all, I did pretty well, especially with the first one. The second was a bit forced, but she was already quite satisfied as it was. Naturally it was done wearing 'raincoats'. They brought the 'raincoats' themselves. I suspected they brought them from Japan because they seemed so delicate. One was transparent and the other was red. Had I not worn them (I hate the things), I would probably have performed better. The trick of doing it with this kind of old lady is that once you're in the mood, you can practically do it with your eyes closed. Both seemed to be in a good temper after that, and they began discussing something I couldn't fully understand. Perhaps they were comparing notes. It seemed that they were experts at this sort of thing. Were they having a sex tour of the world? I wondered why Japanese ladies at their age (they had at least a century between them) could be so open. One of them gave me a beer from the refrigerator. I took two mouthfuls and lit a cigarette. I got dressed as I puffed. I wanted to leave that dark room quickly, for it was as oppressive as the feudal society of China's past. They already put the money on the TV set, reminding me that what had happened was not a romantic encounter.

Of course I did not go back to look for that disgusting waiter, I hurried through the lobby of the Castle Hotel and escaped.

The real punishment came later. One day I heard that two old ladies had been murdered at the Castle Hotel. I knew that the police would come looking for me any minute. I had left too many traces in that room that night. I even wondered whether the thin tall waiter also had a hand in it. Yet the police never came, even after three days. Still, I knew that they would come eventually. It was then I made the sudden decision to go home. In reality I did not go back straight away. Instead I went to work in Zhuhai for six months before heading home. By then I received news from a classmate in Xi'an that the case had been resolved.

'Have you finished the story?'

'Yes.'

'I want to ask you a question. Do you still write poetry?'

'You may not remember, but you asked me this question earlier this evening. I don't write poetry any more, no. I gave it up a long time ago.'

'Are you writing fiction then?'

'No, I don't even have enough time to take care of my business, let alone write fiction.'

'You don't understand. I am saying that you have the talent for fiction. It's a pity you don't.'

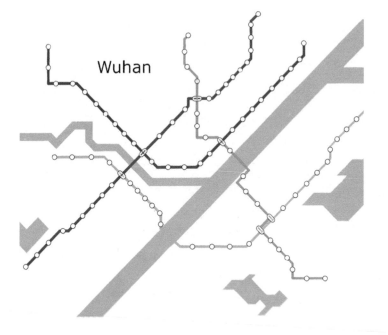
Wuhan

Dear Wisdom Tooth

ZHANG ZHIHAO

TRANSLATED BY JOSH STENBERG

LUO MA CAN remember the first time my wisdom tooth started acting up. That was twelve years ago, and we had only been going steady for a little while. It was late autumn, and campus was infused with the scent of aloeswood, what's called the 'sinking aroma'. The osmanthus was beginning its second bloom, before the fragrance of the first had entirely dissipated. We left the library, and walked along the street for about a hundred meters before turning into a little roadside grove. We kept stopping to kiss as we walked, looking like two very clumsy brown bears. Afterwards, we stopped by a stout old camphor tree. 'You began to unbutton my blouse. Then you suddenly stopped,' said Luo Ma. 'That was the first time your wisdom tooth acted up.'

Well, then when was the second time? I was holding my aching right cheek, half of my face was already numb. I had taken three Ibuprofens half an hour before, and now they were having their effect.

'We went for a spring outing to South Lake. You found a stick of bamboo somewhere, and made a fish hook out of a brooch I was wearing, and then you tied the hook on the rod with both your shoelaces. I caught some grasshoppers in the meadow, while you sat on the shore and fished. All you caught that morning was a handful of lake shrimp. In the afternoon, you finally landed a carp. It was the ugliest fish I had ever seen, so much so that I even doubted whether it was a real fish at all, or just some illusion. You were happy as a little kid that day, barefoot, your trouser-legs rolled way up high, jumping up and down and all around the lakeshore…'

Don't go off on a tangent. What happened then?

'Later, you found some firewood, and we grilled the fish and the shrimp by the shore and ate them all up.'

What about after that?

After we were finished eating, we still didn't want to head back to campus. It was getting dark out. You took my hand and led me into a little patch of rapeseed. It was May, and the rapeseed blossoms made a kind of golden carpet, which shone in the dusk with a peculiar lustre. We were like two bees, hot on each other's heels through the flowers. You tripped me and I fell to the ground in the centre of the rapeseed patch. You pressed me down, you were like a wild animal. With practiced hand, you took off my top, and because you had unfastened it many times before, you knew where to find the hook on my bra. Then you began to take off my pants. I was wearing jeans that day, the tight, form-fitting kind. And this is where your inexperience proved an obstacle, because you just couldn't get them off, and had to ask me for help. But when I was down to my undies, you just stopped…'

What happened?

'It was your wisdom tooth! It started acting up just in time. It saved me.'

What do you mean by that?

'Nothing. Think about it, if it weren't for your wisdom tooth, I would have lost my maidenly honour. So I ought to feel grateful towards it.'

You seem to be saying that if it weren't for my wisdom tooth, you wouldn't be the person you are today. Is that it? But have you considered that something of the sort was likely to happen sooner or later; and didn't you lose it to me in the end anyway?

'You're not a woman, you don't understand how

important that sort of thing is to us. Did you think it was just some kind of rite of passage? Not at all. It's a promise. If I give it to you, it means I've decided to entrust my whole life to you. But if you try to get it by force, then it's a demand, an act of possession. The two end results are totally different.'

I still didn't really get it. Luo Ma's explanation seemed a bit of a stretch, and I'd have said a little contradictory. My take on this is that a woman who is loved has the right to choose when and where she wants to be petted, but since the man in question has already decided to spend his life with you, there's no need to play coy or wait. Especially when Luo Ma herself took off those form-fitting jeans. At the time, she could totally have refused. She could have reacted like those other two girls I had met before, shoving me firmly away, or even giving me a resounding slap in the face. In many situations, a good slap can clear your head, although of course there are also examples to the contrary; but not in my case. I'm a straightforward, above-board kind of guy, or at least I was then. But see, she shimmied out of her jeans herself. I can still remember her expression just then: her eyes glazed, her cheeks scarlet, and she was panting. Her hands were trembling, and her pelvis slightly raised, so that the butt-hugging jeans could slip over her generous hips, her knees bent, and as the belt-buckle grazed her calves, she wore an expression of staunch resolution.

'I suppose you haven't forgotten Wang Qiang. Frankly, if I had given myself to you then, I would probably now be his wife, and not yours.'

The more you say, the more confused I get. I patted my swollen cheeks and went on: I've heard of women staying chaste for a man they love, but I've never heard of a woman giving her virginity to a man she didn't love.

'Well, that's a given. Even I haven't figured out what exactly I was thinking just then. I went to high school with Wang Qiang, and then after that to university. The truth is he could easily have gone to a better university. But when we filled out our preferences, he took a look at my form, and asked me what I thought. I told him to do whatever. So that's how he became my classmate at university, too. I said to myself, if all of life were nothing but education and schooling, Wang Qiang would be my classmate forever. I could see what his intentions were, as clear as day. His problem was that he was too chicken. I even once tried to give him some subtle encouragement, but he just shrunk back even more. And then I said yes to you. Said I'd go out with you. And every time we went out on a date I'd go to him and report: that guy kissed me yesterday; today he touched my breasts... I pretty much didn't leave anything out – I told him everything. And he'd look at me, dumbstruck, blushing to the roots of his hair; as if the guy kissing me, touching me, wasn't you at all, as if it were all him. I knew that he was just that kind of person, he had too much self-respect, and was as stubborn as a mule. That kind of a man is an absolute rock in marriage, but he's not exactly prime cut when it comes to love. That's what I was thinking, back then, thinking, I can give my love to you, and give marriage to him, give you my maiden effort, but keep my mature work for him. That seemed the only thing I could do, in order to have it both ways...'

With the result that your maiden effort was severely delayed, am I right? It's all very strange.

'What I want to know is, why did you stay away from me after that? Since you already knew that I wouldn't say no, even if you came right out and asked for it, then why didn't you want it anymore, afterwards?'

The wisdom tooth. It was all because of my tooth.

'Because of your tooth? How so?'

You remember how you guys left town just before graduation, to fulfil your practical experience requirement? While you were gone, I had another bad time of it with my wisdom tooth. It was worse this time: fierce, sudden attacks, just mind-blowing, churning waves of pain, one after the other. I went to the army hospital and met an army dentist

there. I mean it sounds really formal to call her an army
dentist, actually she was just this girl, although a little more
mature than most girls, so I guess she was like something
between a virgin and a woman. Properly speaking, she ought
to be called a young lady. She was really pretty – I had just
never seen a woman that graceful before. She examined my
teeth. That day, she was dressed in a full-length white lab coat,
with a surgical mask that resolutely covered her face. I was
lying on that damned dentist's chair, lifting my head, looking
at the twinkle in her great big eyes. Suddenly, I thought of a
detail I had read in a war novel – an injured soldier, a white-
gowned angel, the soldier's about to die, he begs the white-
gowned angel to give him a kiss. And when I thought of
myself as that dying soldier, a strange, happy feeling surged
through my heart. Then, when she was done with my gums,
she sat down on the edge of a chair. She took off her mask.
Her beauty made me forget all my pain. But she was calm as
anything, I guess she was used to seeing expressions like the
one I had on my face. She motioned for me to sit up, jotted
something down in my records, and got straight to asking me
all sorts of stuff. When she found out that I still hadn't
graduated from university, she raised her head and glanced at
me. Is that so? she said, like she didn't quite believe me. Yes, I
said, but hastened to add, I've almost graduated, but not just
yet. She glanced at me once more, but then dropped her head
and didn't look me in the eye until I went to see her again the
next day. So you came, she said in a nondescript tone, not at
all surprised. Before coming I had brushed my teeth and
chewed gum all the way over. I lay down and opened my
mouth. I was very nervous, because she had told me the day
before that if the inflammation had gone down, she was going
to pull my tooth today. I lay there motionless, thinking that
when she came over beside me I absolutely had to ask her to
kiss my forehead. But I waited practically forever and she still
hadn't come over. She had left me out to dry, on the freezing
iron-frame bed, while she was off on the side, noisily fussing

about with something. All I could hear was the whirr of some machine, but I couldn't even catch a glimpse of her. She did finally come over to stand right in front of me, shining the lamp in my mouth. Are you chewing gum? She asked. Yes, I replied, like I had done something really shameful. You shouldn't be, she said. Anything sugary will aggravate your internal organ heat, and stimulate oral mucus. Here, let me take a good look. With her tweezers, she tugged the corner of my mouth aside, and bent over to look in, and said, no way, there's not a chance of it today, keep taking the medicine for another couple of days. I was a bit disappointed – the disappointment felt by the condemned inmate who's made all his preparations to take the big leap and but then told they've commuted the sentence to indefinite imprisonment: a sudden, hollow feeling. I pleaded with her, please, just do it, I can't wait any longer. But she shook her head resolutely. Come back the day after tomorrow, she said.

After two days, I went to her the third time. Without asking anyone's permission, I just walked right up to that dentist's chair and lay down in it. This time, she showed no hesitation, and approached my mouth decisively. She stood with one leg on either side of my body, and my knees brushed against hers. Because the weather was already very hot, I was only wearing shorts, and as for her, she just had a skirt on underneath her lab coat. When she spread her legs, standing in front of me, I pushed my ass up and was almost touching her hips, and my body began to pulse back and forth. She commanded me, open your mouth! I don't know where I got the courage from, but I stretched out my arm and lifted the mask from her mouth. You're so beautiful! I gasped in admiration. You can admire me later, she said. No, later I won't have the energy left to admire you, I just have to tell you, I said, I beg of you! What do you beg of me, she said, brushing my hand away and taking a comfy seat on my thigh…

'That's disgusting! You have some nerve! How could you be such a slimeball!'

Well, that's why I always felt uneasy about it later. But I

swear, I never went back to see her again. She gave me her phone number, but I never called. It's OK. If our relationship is over, we might as well just have it all out.

'But I never did anything I'm ashamed of, not like you. To go by your face, you seem trustworthy enough, but inside you're nothing but filth!'

Give me a break. You mean to tell me there was nothing like that going on between you and Wang Qiang? I said disdainfully. Because of all the talking I'd been doing my tooth started to ache and my mood took a turn for the worse.

'Nothing.'

Well then, how can you explain what happened between you and Zhang Chao? Stop blushing, there's nothing embarrassing about that whole thing, I mean look at us, it's not like I'm going to raise a fuss about all that now. I propped my chin up on my right arm, my hand covering my face, my five fingers constantly pushing on the gums. Numbed pain is even worse than the ordinary kind.

'Zhang Chao? What are you bringing him up for? It's been a long time since I had anything to say about what happened that night.'

But I have something to say. Essentially, what you did with him isn't any different from what I did with the dentist. Since I've already confessed everything, there's nothing for you to be worried about.

'Of course there isn't. I've told you, I was drunk.'

And therefore you had to go to bed with some guy? That's an extraordinary theory.

'Anyhow, if you hadn't had the pain in your wisdom tooth, if you had been there drinking with us, and I got wasted – but you had been there – then none of all that would ever have happened. But halfway through you got up and ran off, and said you were going to see a dentist, although for all any of us knew you were going after some other woman. Who the hell knows! Anyway, when I woke up I was lying on a huge hotel bed, without a stitch on me. I didn't take my own clothes off – your wife was forcibly stripped naked, but you weren't too bothered. Not only did you fail to go settle accounts with the guy, but the only thing you were good for was to turn the air blue. And when it was over, weren't you two still as thick as thieves? And didn't you get that engineering project you wanted from him, then? And besides, didn't you have a certain thing for his wife? That's right, what about you and his wife, afterwards?'

Well, I slept with her.

'How did you get her into bed?'

So I took over that project from Zhang Chao. Usually Zhang Chao wasn't at home. But I often went to his place, and just sat and chatted with her on any pretext at all. In the end she reluctantly acquiesced. But I paid a high price for it. I only earned seventy or eighty grand on that project, but I spent fifty or sixty on his wife, which is to say that I worked for a month for next to nothing. Afterwards, I thought that we were quits, since we had each done the other's wife. The problem was, although I had ten, twenty in surplus and revenue, that's without taking into account all the time I wasted on the project. Of course, it was a consolation that while Zhang Chao had only nailed you once, and when you were passed out, I had done his wife at least a dozen times, and always when she was perfectly sober...

'You men make wild animals look good. I guess now I've really seen through you jerks.'

Why don't we change the subject? I said, Let's talk about our ten years of married life, through thick and thin. How about that?

'There's not much to say about it, and you can forget about thick and thin. It was a mistake; a mistake as plain as the nose on your face.'

I don't think so; no matter how it ends, we've been a loving couple through the years. Like for instance, every time my wisdom tooth aches: who else but you takes me to the airport, nags me to take my medicine according to schedule, serves me congee, and runs around asking people to find out what miracle cure there might be for wisdom tooth pain? Except for that one time you mentioned, you're the one who takes care of me every time it happens.

Like they say: a dying bird sings a sad song. That's the sad state you're in. Why does everything have to come to an end before you look back and see how good you had it? And when the time comes to look back, why are our hearts filled with remorse and anger? Why is it always like this? Do you still remember that poem you wrote – I forget what you called it, but I remember some of the lines:

> Everywhere you went leaving footprints of a beast
> The life you doubted is still the trap towards which
> The majority swarms, there, a tiger
> Setting off on a journey, a crowd of children
> Trying to buy the skin off his back,
> There, the snow falls, life is wary.

'That's true. Through the years we have lived warily, afraid of hurting each other, but actually continually doing just that. Maybe you wanted to be that tiger, setting off on a journey, while I was trying to buy the skin off a tiger's back – a hopeless pursuit. And really so tiring. That's why I want to say that an ending like this isn't really such a bad thing.'

You're right, it's not such a bad thing, I sighed. I picked up a nearby little medicine kit and started rummaging about inside it. There were all kinds of medical supplies in it, but most of them had something to do with toothaches. I once made a very solemn vow that once the swelling had gone down I would go straight to the dentist's and have my wisdom tooth out, but whenever the ache was over, I would forget all about it and let the solemn vow go to the devil. I can still remember what that first lady dentist had said to me. She had said, 'This wisdom tooth here isn't going to grow out, it's what we call impacted, the only thing to do is to pull it out.'

I remember she didn't actually use the ordinary word

'pull', she said 'dig.' 'Dig it out!' She said, gesturing energetically up and down, up and down. Later, I went to a number of different dentists, and they all drew more or less the same conclusion: dig it out, not pull it out. Naturally it was perfectly clear to me the significance of, and difference between, these two verbs. Any digging would certainly involve its surroundings, and if they got too involved, then the cure would be worse than the illness. That's why, despite my solemn vows, in my heart I still tended towards a conservative course of treatment. Luo Ma mocked my cowardice, my lack of spirit or boldness. But she was only half-right. Maybe I did lack a bold spirit, but what the hell is a bold spirit good for? No good at all. At university, I happened to read a book that said all the organs of the human body belonged to God and were gifts from your parents, so that any human extraction was an unrighteous action. I accepted this account of things, and that the absolute crux of preserving the self was to preserve every part of my body, no matter how large or how small, useful or useless; that everything should be preserved as much as possible, unless God intervened to exact it from me. A few years ago, when I had appendicitis, the doctor advised me to have it out. 'It's useless, why keep it!' The doctor said. But I couldn't bring myself to have it out. I believe that a loving and righteous human being ought to act with love and righteousness towards his own body, otherwise, all the human ties of love and righteousness are nothing but hot air.

'What are you looking for?'

Painkillers. I said, where did you put all the painkillers?

'Are you trying to kill yourself? You just gobbled up all those Ibuprofens, and now you want the painkillers. Seriously, are you trying to kill yourself? Look, why don't I take you to the hospital and put you on the IV drip?'

Forget it. I was still stooped over the medicine kit, its contents scattered all over the place: white tablets, green tablets. Pain is a monster running roughshod. I've known that since I was very little, because of my mother. She had headaches her whole life long: first it was ordinary headaches, later migraines, and finally they turned into full-fledged nervous headaches. Every time the monster got near my mother, I could see her scrambling about, trying to find some weapon to ward it off. Mother's weapon was a bag of inexpensive headache powder. I can still remember the picture on that paper bag: a man holding his forehead in both hands, looking desperate and hopeless. But this inexpensive weapon helped my mother through many a night, twisting and turning in bed. The strange thing was that what Mum died of didn't have anything to do with her chronic headaches. She died of cancer of the nose and throat – another subtle, crafty monster. Looking at it that way, headaches were simply the external appearance of my mother's life, while the truth was securely concealed for years underneath the unremitting pain. And it is also from this perspective that I realized that the wisdom tooth was to me what headaches were to my mother, and that I had to be endlessly vigilant against any of these monsters which adhere to one's insides. I suppose that toothaches are just the camouflage these monsters habitually employ, while the actual suffering is behind the physical pain. But what is the suffering? A few days ago, I kept turning this question over in my head.

'Maybe, you could try to take another couple of anti-inflammatories. Do you have any amoxicillin left? Of course, no matter what, you mustn't take too many of them; they'll damage your nerves. Here you are, but you can only have four for today.'

I grabbed them out of her hands and stuffed them into my mouth.

'I think, after what you've been through this time, you should make up your mind and have it pulled.'

Dug out, not pulled, I corrected.

'Like it matters. In any case it'll be removed from your body.'

Easy for you to say, I replied, but have you thought about what's going to fill the space it leaves, after it's been dug out?

'Well, when I leave, who do you intend to fill the space I leave behind?'

After all we've said, you're still singing the same old tune. Having a tooth pulled is one thing, and getting a divorce is another. Why do you keep mixing them up together, what are you getting at?

'Nothing.'

What do you mean by nothing?

'By nothing I mean nothing. Don't you get it? A smart guy like you, you can't even figure that out?'

But I couldn't. Luo Ma said I was smart, but in that case I don't know where my intelligence is keeping itself. I'm a moron. From the very first day I had the ache in my wisdom tooth, I've been a hostage to pain; pain has drilled me into a bona fide moron, which is not the sort of thing you can fake. In every year there's always a few days or patches where I walk through the crowds, holding my cheek, while fashionable men and women go past me on the street, walking in pairs, and everything is like a great cauldron of steaming, vibrant life. But me, even though I'm drooling with desire, I just pretend like I'm totally unaffected, in my suit and leather shoes, a briefcase under my arm, never casting a sideways glance. I set store in keeping face. Another man's slept with my wife and I keep it quiet. I'd rather blow my cash on getting the other guy's wife into bed than confronting him in public. If that's what you call smart, then the Earth must be empty of fools.

'Just have it pulled, it's for the best.'

Dug, I corrected her again. Dug out, not pulled.

'I asked the doctor, and he said, although anti-inflammatories can control the progression, if you look at the question long-term, having it pulled is definitely better than holding off, because it's very likely that it's damaging your gums, and if that takes a bad turn you could get an oral cyst...'

Which is mouth cancer, right? I interrupted her, and

went on: I'd rather trust anyone in the whole world than a doctor. All they're good for is scaremongering, but as soon as they come up against some kind of tricky disease, they all throw up their hands and give up.

'The problem with you is that you're suspicious of everything. You're supposed to be some kind of intellectual, and ought to know that the primary thing in getting along with people is having good faith. You have to believe in me. And what's believing in people? It's trust. In China, we only pay attention to the one side of trust: credibility. But we often ignore the power of the other aspect of trust, which is reliance. That's why everything here is so lawless, because we hold nothing sacred. It's entirely different from how things are in Western countries. I used to think foreign films were so weird. Someone puts their hand on the Bible in court and then they can't perjure themselves. In our lives here that would be just nuts...'

You could put a knife to his throat, and he'd still be telling fairy tales.

'Exactly. Why is that? Because we don't believe. And the prerequisite for not believing is being suspicious like you, suspicious of the doctors' skills. And you imagine you can find some way out of it all – you'll wriggle out of the pain and suffering somehow, am I right? That's what it seems like to me. Besides, if you don't believe in medicine, then why did you go to that lady dentist, anyway?'

Not that again. I waved her off impatiently: Can't you talk about something that'll take my mind off the pain? I asked.

'Probably not. You know, we are surrounded by suffering, you and I. It's the same for both of us.'

Then just shut up, I shouted, and in a way that relieved the accumulated frustration and rage of the last few days, at least. I'm sorry, I said, apologizing right away, that was just because of the tooth.

'What you really mean is, it was just because of our

marriage, since that hateful wisdom tooth you've got buried deep inside you is really me.'

Piss off!! I was really angry. My nose was already out of joint, but that really ticked me off.

'Swear as much as you like. In any case after tonight I won't ever be able to hear you swearing.'

My married life with Luo Ma had proceeded as a constant series of fights. It was like a man and a woman had gotten into a car to go visit some godforsaken scenic area, and the road was really bumpy, which was completely exhausting, but they thought that when they were through this rough patch they would get to the smooth and level road. But that was only a dream, they never got to a really smooth and level road – just the contrary. The further they traveled, the narrower it got, and the legendary scenic area was still unthinkably far away. I had lost patience already. And I knew that Luo Ma was just the same: she didn't have any hope left for future prospects.

May as well have it pulled, I said, clenching my teeth. I didn't know whether Luo Ma had heard me, because the thought growing in my mind had seemed very loud, but when I actually said it I was clenching my teeth, so it probably come out all shredded.

'What are you mumbling on about?'

She really hadn't heard me clearly. When it gets light out, I'll go to the hospital and have the fucking tooth pulled, I said.

'Dug out, not pulled.'

I watched Luo Ma, sitting on the sofa, starting to snicker. I had to admit, Luo Ma looked amazing when she laughed. It was her laugh, like a net, that had caught me and dragged me to her side. I had to admit that of all the women I had met to date, Luo Ma was the one best suited to me – not the most beautiful, but absolutely the most suitable. And I also had to admit, even now when our marriage had run its course, that I was very fond of her. I had to admit as well that having lost

Luo Ma I would spend a long period of time wallowing in remorse. Luo Ma was the only one. Luo Ma was irreplaceable. I sometimes thought if Luo Ma had not married me but Wang Qiang instead or some other guy, our relationship might be one suffused with sweet memories; we might arrange trysts somewhere on the sly, coming together only to part again, maintaining our clandestine love until the end of our days. I remember when we were newly-weds, there had been a joke between us, neither very serious nor the opposite: I had said, what if one day I just got up and left home, and after many years, when my hair was grey, I came back to you — what would you do?

Luo Ma had tapped me over the heart with her index finger and asked, 'Like Wakefield in the Hawthorne story? What do you think I ought to do?'

I had said, if I were you, I'd lock myself up until that man came back. 'I know what you're driving at,' she had laughed. 'You mean to say that real life ought to be able to outlast the ravages of time, to put it simply: to be eighty, and share the same bed! Am I right?' And as she spoke, she sprang suddenly to her feet and pushed me firmly down onto the bed. 'Whatever happened to 'being eighty, and sharing the same bed!' I laughed out loud...

Thinking of it now, it was like we couldn't wait for it to come. Eighty years old — far away! Although the last couple of years did seem to have passed in a flash, eighty still seemed a long way off. Which is to say, both of us still had to endure several times over the misery that we had already endured, until we could finally make it there, and besides, God only knows whether when we're eighty we'll still be able to make love anyway. Two old people sleeping in the same bed are relying on habit, not on love, and besides habit, one also needs courage.

'Sometimes, you're just like a child.'

A child? I repeated this new title uncertainly.

'Right, a kid is just what you are, childish through and

through, otherwise, why would you still have a wisdom tooth at thirty-five?'

Suddenly, I saw what she meant – since in Chinese the characters for 'wisdom' and 'childishness' sound the same, both pronounced *zhi*. So I asked her, do you know how to write wisdom tooth?

'The *zhi* that means childish, and the *chi* that means teeth.'

Wrong! I shouted. I can't believe we've been together so many years and you haven't even figured out what my sickness is all about!

'Am I wrong? Really?'

Of course you're wrong, I said, it's the *zhi* that means wisdom, not the *zhi* that means childish. You really are an airhead.

'I'm sorry.'

According to medical science, wisdom teeth start growing only when a person has acquired some wisdom, hence the name. I explained, Strictly speaking, the question of wisdom teeth ought to be resolved for a normal person by the time he's twenty-four by either letting them grow in, or having them pulled. The problem is that this wisdom tooth of mine is very special, like it's got a problem with me. Sometimes I think it's because my wisdom is not yet complete, but I've been to the hospital all those times, and can you explain why have I never seen airheads getting their wisdom teeth pulled? It goes to show that the medical explanation is far-fetched.

'I'm sorry.'

It honestly had not occurred to me that Luo Ma didn't know which characters we were talking about, just like how all the dentists could talk about having to pull your teeth, but couldn't say why they thought it was imperative to pull them. Between extraction and non-extraction there is a black hole, and you can poke at it with scissors or a chisel or extend a probe light into it, but you can never see the pain; all you can see is a hard object buried in the flesh. That's my wisdom tooth, but it's not only my wisdom tooth. That's my pain, but it's not the origin of my pain.

'I'm sorry that I didn't pay more attention. How do you want me to make it up to you?'

What have you got in mind? I asked, What could you do now?

'What I want to do most is to dance with you one more time to 'Say You, Say Me'.'

I pulled back the sheets and rolled out of bed. I could already hear the touching, gentle melody in the living room. Actually, the melody had been running around in my head for years, but because the toothache was such a distraction, I hadn't really been listening.

'Ready?'

I cleaned myself up and dressed in front of the mirror. I decided to give myself a new start, inside and out. I changed my underpants and shirt, and over the snow-white dress shirt I wore a coffee-brown tie, and over that a crisp suit. After a quick once-over, I went to the bathroom and brushed my teeth despite the terrific pain, and even gently scraped off the stubble on my chin with a Gillette razor blade. I dawdled, wishing that time could freeze at that instant. My heart was beating fast, and my cheeks flushed a deep red. I heard a hoarse, magnetic voice playing in the guest room, heard my heart pulsing like a stream through a crevice. But I knew I had to go out, because on this CD, 'Tears On My Pillow' would be up next, and then came 'I've Never Been to Me,' which is even sadder.

I opened the door, and heard Luo Ma whisper into my ear, 'Come on, my dear wisdom tooth!'

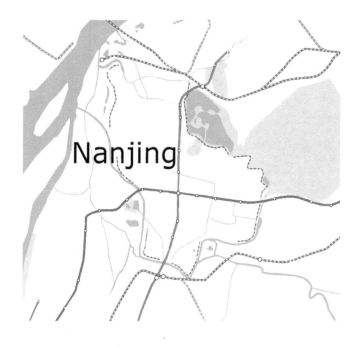

This Moron is Dead

HAN DONG

TRANSLATED BY NICKY HARMAN

A MAN WAS lying on the pavement. He was dead.

There were lots of people coming and going. This was where the number 31 bus stopped for the Cockcrow Nunnery and there was a stop for the number 11, 16 and 1 bus as well.

When people first noticed him, they took him for some sort of a permanent fixture. He wasn't exactly an improvement to the environment, but neither was he offensive. Like a fire hydrant, he could just be ignored.

Of course, they didn't really feel that when someone died in the street, they should just be left there unburied. They weren't totally devoid of compassion. It was just that they weren't sure if he was dead – he might just be having a bit of a rest. There were plenty of people who didn't care what anyone thought of them and didn't give tuppence for traffic regulations. That meant they could lead completely carefree lives. Maybe this man was just having a nice sleep.

So if people stepped around him, careful not to touch him or stare too hard, it was out of respect for a different way of life. Of course some of them regarded him with disdain, but I think mostly they ignored him because they were afraid of being distracted as they rushed to get on and off their buses. A few, however, had to pass that way several times during the day and, by the second or third time, they couldn't help being surprised that he was still lying there completely motionless.

And those who had to spend the whole day there, because of their jobs, certainly felt a little uneasy about him.

Like the old woman who sat outside the public toilet collecting the entry fee, the young man in the photographic studio, or the traffic control officer who directed traffic at the crossroads fifty yards away. To varying degrees, as the hours passed, they all found their attention drawn to this strange man. Then there were the flies, which had begun to pay him frequent visits.

It was the flies that alerted people to the oddness of this man. The old woman was surprised that there were fewer flies than usual in the toilet; that useless beggar must have tempted them away. Those cute little flies belonged to her, they came with the job. And now she could only watch, green with envy, as they deserted her for him. She wanted to chase him away and win her flies back. She went over and shouted at him.

The man did not answer, so the old woman gave him a kick. The arm, which had until now rested on his head, slid off, revealing an ashen face. The old woman gave a cry – and this told everyone immediately that the man was dead.

He had finally got a reaction. But it was short-lived. An old man among the bystanders felt he should do the decent thing and cover this terrible sight up with something. He had a good look around, but found nothing.

It was astonishing just how civilised the city was becoming. The street was a hundred years old, yet apart from the cherry blossom petals which littered the ground, there was absolutely nothing suitable. People threw their fruit stones and the like into the rubbish bins, and litterbugs were much frowned upon nowadays. The old man sighed and shook his head sadly. Then he thought of the general store around the corner; he would go and ask the shopkeeper for an old cardboard box.

The boxes may have been old but they were still saleable. There were three universities nearby and the shopkeeper often sold them to the students at one *yuan* a box. They used them to pack their textbooks and other odds and ends in. This was the best business he did so he wasn't going to give them away. The old man knew that two cardboard boxes would be needed but, when he asked, the shop owner replied: 'What's so special about a dead body? If you want boxes, buy them.'

The old man protested that the dead man was not a relative or a friend. Why would he want to go spending money on him?

The shop owner did not want an argument and sold him one box half-price. Then he told his wife to watch the shop and went back with him to take a look.

The old man tore the box open and placed it over the dead man's face. There was nothing to cover the rest of the body with so it had to remain exposed to view. He stepped back to admire his handiwork. He really had made a difference.

But with the face covered up, the moron looked even less like a corpse, and more like a tramp taking a nap and using the cardboard as a sun-shield. This would be a misunderstanding; the old man started to worry that the corpse would be mistaken for a living person. And he wondered what he had died of. Anyone who went too close might catch it off him.

The old man felt a prickling in his finger; he had the urge to write something on the cardboard, to alert passers-by. Just then, a young man standing nearby, who might have been an artist, pulled a chunky marker pen out of his pocket and handed it over with the words: 'Feel free to use this.' The old man took it and fiddled with it for a while: 'The ink certainly smells strong.'

Before committing himself to the cardboard, he had a practice on a piece of old newspaper. 'I haven't written anything for so long, I'm afraid you'll find I have a very poor hand,' he said. 'Of course not,' the youth reassured him.

The old man considered the wording of the notice carefully. He felt the young artist was the only person with any education (at least, judging by the very fine pen he had on him), so he consulted him. But they couldn't come up with anything. Then he tried the toilet attendant, who knew everything about everyone. 'He was a moron,' she said. 'Never right in the head.'

'Ah, I know just what to say!' said the old man. And with much swishing of the marker pen, he wrote on the cardboard: *This moron is dead.*

The bystanders gasped in admiration at his calligraphy. 'It's nothing,' said the old man deprecatingly. 'Now if I had a calligraphy brush, *then* you could judge my writing.'

The artist continued the old man's work by getting a piece of chalk out of his breast pocket. (It was astonishing the number of writing implements he had on him). He drew a large chalk circle on the pavement around the moron's head. This required no skill at all. He just had to make sure that the ends more or less joined up. The effect of the circle was instantly to exclude all the bystanders. Then he left, followed by those onlookers who had been there longest; they all rushed off to catch their buses. Only the moron carried on lying there as before, with the addition of a cardboard box on his head. People took even less notice of him than before, except for the flies, which enthusiastically stuck around him. They swarmed in intricate patterns over the body. 'Good-for-nothings!' the toilet attendant swore at them. 'You'll go anywhere for a bit of rotting meat!' If she hadn't been so loyal to her work, she would have upped sticks and stomped indignantly away. Too bad the toilets could not be moved. She just had to carry on sitting there feeling rejected.

Half an hour later, two young boys chased each other across the road. The one in front was looking behind him, stumbled over the body and almost went head over heels. He righted himself by putting one foot nimbly on the body and was running on, when his friend stopped:

'You just touched a dead body.' Then he went slowly up to the white chalk circle and looked at the notice: 'He's a moron,' he said. 'He's dead,' said the other boy.

They argued over the writing on the card, neither prepared to give way, until each was red in the face. Finally, they came to an agreement: this really was a moron but he was dead. So he was a dead moron.

Then the boy who had arrived first said: 'Just now I kicked him.' He seemed to feel this gave him an advantage over his taller friend.

'That was an accident,' objected the other. 'I bet you don't dare touch him now!'

'Course I do!' said the smaller boy. But he hesitated and the pair stood facing each other with the moron between them. The smaller boy was suspicious that he might be tricked by his friend if he came any closer, and also worried his friend might be more afraid than him.

'I'm not afraid,' said the smaller boy. He stepped into the chalk circle and gave the cardboard box a kick. That brought him nearer to the smaller boy, who involuntarily took a step back.

'You scared?!' the other jeered. 'Scared of a dead man? A moron?'

'Course not! I can stand here for as many minutes as you!' the smaller boy insisted.

The contest between them was beginning to draw a crowd but no one paid much attention to the dead man; it was the boys' boldness which made them gasp with admiration. 'When we were young, we were such innocents compared with kids nowadays!'

By now the bigger boy had given up the chase; he stood inside the circle, counting the seconds in a loud voice. The smaller one, green with jealousy at his friend's sudden celebrity, forgot his fears, stepped into the circle and pushed his friend out. 'I can stand here as many minutes as you!' he repeated.

The bigger boy, not wanting to be left out, immediately stepped back in, and the pair stood rigid as doorposts until finally the bystanders began to lose interest and drifted away. Only the boys and the moron were left at the roadside. Then, at almost the same moment, they suddenly remembered that they'd been chasing each other. The smaller boy stepped out of the circle and made a dash for it, with the bigger boy in hot pursuit. Their shouts faded into the distance.

Once more, the moron was left with only flies for company.

I got off the minibus at about four in the afternoon. All the people getting off saw the moron but no one was interested enough to hang around. I would probably have walked away just like them, if I hadn't been meeting my girlfriend. It so happened that our meeting place was precisely the spot where the moron had expired.

I waited and waited but my girlfriend didn't turn up. She always was a slowcoach, but it was unusual for her to be as late as she was today.

I was almost pathological about sticking to my word, so I didn't dare budge from where we'd arranged to meet. Since the moron had occupied what was normally my place, I had to stand by the wall three paces away with my eyes fixed on him. Or rather, fixed on the regular spot where I met my girlfriend. That meant that, as the minutes crawled by, I had to keep looking at the moron. I could see one bare calf, well-muscled and quite hairy. As good as my own, really. The flies droned around, continually taking off and landing as I watched. The only difference between the moron and me was that his skin was a blue-grey colour while mine was still pinky-white, which was something to be grateful for. Then I noticed the indifference of the people passing by. Why was no one even glancing in his direction, except me?

There had always been plenty to gawp at on this street corner. That was probably why we frequented it and made it our meeting place. Every day there were scuffles and squabbles, a petty thief being collared by a policeman, and so on. I'm not exaggerating when I say that all this added spice to our love life. I remember one evening, a guy got hit on the head with a brick. So much blood streamed down his face, you couldn't see the wound. It sent my girlfriend into shock. Our lovemaking that night was more intense than ever before, even though we'd almost decided to split up before that. That bloody episode saved our relationship. I bet there are plenty of other people out there who benefitted the same way that night.

Maybe the moron was just too quiet. He lay there inert – and nothing happened. He wasn't so much an event as an image, a symbol which made no sense and which didn't need to make sense. He was just boring. People are creatures of feeling and instinct, increasingly unaccustomed to investigating things properly. We only react to movement and understand what we live through.

Just as these thoughts were flitting through my head, a blond, blue-eyed foreigner turned up. An exquisitely pretty compatriot of mine sat on his shoulders. They stopped in front of the moron. I couldn't help thinking to myself: that's a foreigner, and they've got God. Surely he won't ignore someone who's lying dead in the street, will he? I pricked up my ears. The foreigner muttered something. I didn't understand a word. As for his Chinese girlfriend, I could understand her only too well. She was explaining the four characters written on the cardboard. The first and the last two caused her no problem, but the second, 'moron', seemed to take a lot of explaining.

The character for 'moron', she was telling him, was the same character and pronounced the same as the word 'to hang around' but meant something different. It was a noun, meaning 'idiot' or 'feeble-minded', someone who 'wasn't all there'. The foreigner nodded happily, thrilled to have acquired a new Chinese word. He kept repeating it in a strange singsong voice: '…moron, idiot, hang around here. The moron hangs around here… *Daizi daizai zheli.*' The Chinese girl clapped her hands at his cleverness, and they threw their arms around each other in front of the moron, making squelchy kissing noises. As their lips drew apart, they chorused:

'…The moron hangs around here… The moron hangs around here… *Daizi daizai zheli.*'

And off they went in great glee.

'Morons!' exclaimed the old woman toilet attendant, to their retreating backs. I realised I hadn't been the only one watching them.

For a long time I stared after them, sunk in thought. 'Moron!' Suddenly I felt a handbag hit me, and looked up to see my girlfriend. I had been staring in the direction she had come from. She had walked right up to me, and I hadn't noticed.

'What are you looking at? Is that foreigner's girlfriend so pretty?' she asked teasingly. She completely ignored the moron under the cardboard box. That was because she was looking at me, just as I hadn't seen her because I'd been staring so hard at the foreigner and his Chinese girl. It all depended on where your concentration was focused. I smiled apologetically, then grumbled: 'How come you're so late?' I knew she'd say it was right and proper for a girl to be late. I was still disappointed when she said it though.

Then she made some more excuses: 'I had to change my clothes and put on a bit of make-up. Otherwise I'd be outshone by the beautiful cherry blossom!'

That was when I remembered the reason why we were meeting today – to take pictures. As soon as the trees were in flower, lovers of natural beauty all flocked here to be photographed in front of them. They'd been in flower for a few days now. The blossom was another reason for making this the place where we always met. Once a year, we came to take photographs – we must have been coming for seven or eight years now. Cherry was the flower of our love, and the trees blossomed in our photo album, growing bigger and taller each year. Only, in reality, we had to get the moment exactly right. They were only at their peak once a year, and for a very short time. The flowers would suddenly burst forth, and then, in the space of just a couple of days, they'd all drop to the ground. It made us treasure them all the more. And you could only find them in certain places. In our city, all the cherry trees were concentrated in this one street, thirty or forty of them. During one brief moment of history, a span of no more than ten years, they had all been brought on ships from the islands of Japan. So they were not only beautiful, they were fashionably exotic too. It was this foreignness that made them special to us. Having your picture taken against our native peach or plum blossom just wasn't the same.

Luckily, more and more people who were well informed about such things were coming around to this point of view so we didn't feel we were on our own anymore. Every day, when the cherry blossom was out, each tree was surrounded by seventy or eighty people strolling to and fro, taking pictures, and exclaiming in admiration. It was no exaggeration to say that the cherry blossom had become a magnet for Nanjingers, the new thing to do.

Carrying the camera, I led my girlfriend over to a tree smothered in pinky-white flowers. It was nearly dusk and there was little time left. We had to be quick. Through the viewfinder, she was uncommonly beautiful – how had I failed to remember that simple fact when I was standing on the street waiting for her? I think love had something to do with it. The cherry blossom was unimportant. It was my girlfriend who dazzled me. If she wasn't around, the blossom would simply leave me cold. Its sole purpose was to add its radiance to hers.

As the realisation hit me, my eyes blurred with tears. I had to keep my right eye open to get the best shot, so my grateful tears could only drip from my squinting left eye. It was so important to re-examine and renew our love once every year. We mustn't let the occasion slip; it would keep us together for the whole of the following year.

This thought energized me, and it was a warning I gave myself. As I hurriedly took the photographs, I made sure to put my former gloomy thoughts behind me.

Through the viewfinder, I took another look at the moron. He was extraordinarily beautiful too. For instance, when I first looked at his bare leg, I had only seen the flies but now I noticed the flower petals which had fallen on it. Of course I had to be sure my girlfriend did not turn around and see them as well. They were lovely, but not as lovely as the blossom still on the tree branches. She was a sensitive girl, and I did not want her to be distressed by the fact that they had dropped off.

The next day, my girlfriend came flying over, beside herself with rage, and flung the prints down on my table. 'Look! They're all ruined!' In every single one of the thirty-six pictures, there was something else as well as her and the cherry blossom. Those terrible words: 'This moron is dead.'

'Whatever were you thinking of, getting that cardboard box in the picture?!' It was a good thing she hadn't looked to see what was under the cardboard.

I said I really hadn't meant to, it was an accident. I said we would go and take some more pictures the following morning. 'I guarantee there won't be a cardboard box in them next time,' I told her.

We went the next day. The cardboard box and the moron had disappeared, of course – but so had the cherry blossom. There was not a single flower left on the trees. Overnight they had all fallen, leaving just branches bare of everything except for a few leaves.

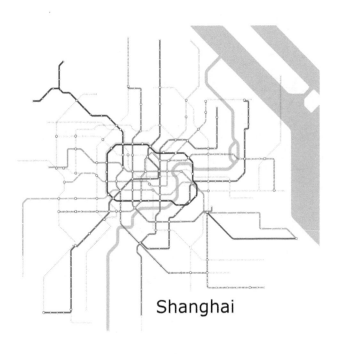

Shanghai

Family Secrets

DING LIYING

TRANSLATED BY NICKY HARMAN

I'M A HOPELESS newspaper columnist, I have to admit. I live on the outskirts of town and every time I go to work, to take phone calls, I can never quite get there on time. I mean, you can't tell what's going to happen on the way, can you? Once I actually saw a three-car pile-up and the car in the middle was scrunched up like a piece of waste paper. I was stuck on the tram with the other passengers for a whole hour. By the time I rushed into the office puffing and panting, I'd used up all my energy in fighting the crowds on the tram and walking the rest of the distance to work.

Today, I got in tired and thirsty, with my trouser-legs rucked up from running. As soon as the lift doors opened, I could see Chen at the far end of the corridor, all ready to go home. He was squatting down in the office doorway, holding a key between his teeth, tying his shoelaces. He had his motorcycle helmet on, and was wearing a long, bulky puffer jacket. The moment he stood up, he looked like an astronaut ready for take-off. I greeted him apologetically: 'I'm late again.'

'That's OK, at least it's only 20 minutes today.' The key dropped out of his mouth as he gave a laugh, but his face was so constricted by the helmet that it looked more like an unpleasant grimace.

'I really am sorry,' I said, pulling out my reporter's notebook, ballpoint pen and stainless steel thermos mug. 'Your girlfriend will be worried.'

'You know what? I always allow an extra hour, or at least half an hour, if I'm meeting someone after work.' He stood upright and did a little karaoke-style jig on the spot. 'I'm used to you, see?'

'I'm really so sorry,' I adjusted my headset and rubbed my hands together.

'Well, I'd better be off,' he pulled on his gauntlets, 'It'll be cold outside.'

'It looks like snow.'

'Can you manage on your own?'

'Yes.'

I watched him disappear into the lift. 'Hey-ho,' I said to myself. 'Everything's fine. I'd better get down to work.' I got up and closed the door, turned up the air conditioning a degree and took off my ski vest.

I was the only one left in the office, and the phone still hadn't rung.

I took a swig of the hot ginseng tea that I had brought with me. I had to admit I was a lousy columnist. Every time I got some overwrought person on the phone, bawling their eyes out or spilling their secrets, I simply didn't know how to handle them. I would sit there paralysed with dismay, taking constant sips of tea or neurotically twisting the phone cable. After each call, I had to remember everything they had told me, and regurgitate it all in the first person, in my column. Some of them sent me letters saying how well I wrote and how I'd helped them get it off their chest. But that wasn't the way I saw myself. I had given myself the pen name Lulu, with the character '*lu*', which means revealing secrets.

I glanced around at the cramped office. There was a wall-mounted air conditioning unit, and a calendar of a pretty seaside scene somewhere abroad. The sky and the water were limpidly clear, and a few holidaymakers were gathering seashells. The figures were so tiny that they appeared far, far away and completely out of reach. The room also held two desks, two revolving chairs, and a filtered water dispenser. A broom and a mop stood in one corner. I sometimes wondered what I was doing in an office like this, taking these messy, hopeless phone calls. Why wasn't I at home with my family – my husband and kid? What on Earth was I doing sitting in this stifling space, listening to these desperately sad stories?

I loathed this job. It felt like being employed to listen to tittle-tattle, like some gossip columnist on a Western tabloid, only interested in other people's scandals. Perhaps I was actually beginning to grow a big nose like a foreigner too. But I had to support myself. My parents lived elsewhere in China and I was on my own. Every month, the rent was 500 yuan, the phone bill 100 yuan, gas and electricity, etc, came to at least 100 yuan. Then there was my life insurance, internet fees and the payments on a fridge and computer. Even if I didn't eat anything at all, the bills still came to over 1,000 yuan a month. I'd had the same lipstick for three years and my disposable contact lenses were almost used up. God, I really needed the money…

Anyway, I did the job just so that I could get by. It really gave me no pleasure. I didn't express my own opinions in my articles, or write with any sympathy. The repulsive stories we printed in the paper seemed to exist independently of me. I never wrote about my feelings or about how astonished I was by the things I heard. Quite honestly, sometimes they seemed unbelievable, but when it came down to it, I always wrote the stories down prosaically and dispassionately.

Once a man phoned to tell me that, ten years previously, he had raped his five-year-old daughter. 'Is that true?' I asked him.

'Of course it is,' he replied. 'But now I've told you the whole story, I've got it off my chest, I've unburdened myself.' But I didn't want him to get it off his chest like that. Another time, a young man called: he'd just had a bust up with his girlfriend and life wasn't worth living any more. He was going to slash his wrists and end it all. My instant reaction was to tell him that slashing your wrists didn't necessarily kill you, and he'd better think of another way. What I meant to say was he shouldn't be in such a hurry to kill himself, why not try and find another girlfriend? He said I was quite right, he'd cut his wrists once and it hadn't worked. So then we mostly talked about whether suicide was really necessary. I was trying to encourage him to want to live again. But two days later, I got a suicide note from him, saying he was going to gas himself instead. I don't know what else I could have said.

Only last Wednesday, just before nine o'clock, a girl phoned to say she was planning to jump from the top of the Jinmao Tower if her boyfriend stood her up that evening. I told her I didn't think the Jinmao Tower had been finished yet. So she said she'd just go out looking for the tallest building in Shanghai she could find. I couldn't be sure what she was going to do but from the sound of her voice, I didn't think it would be anything too terrible. So I didn't pursue it any further. But you see what kind of job I have! They're all stark staring mad. And I always tell them, 'I quite understand the situation you're in,' though actually I don't understand any of it.

I look down at my shoes, count the fine cracks in the uppers, and say to them: 'I completely understand your situation.' But, really, I don't understand a single thing about their lives.

Of course, I always have to take my readers' and the newspaper's tastes into consideration. The article has to have the right effect, so even if I'm seething with indignation, I have to suppress my anger and disgust. Any story that's not strong enough, I edit it so it's a bit more logical and reads better. Of course, this doesn't do the callers any good. In fact, there's no way I can give them any real help. Not only can I not stop these terrible things from happening, I also can't protect anyone from harm, let alone heal their wounds. I really have no idea what to do for them.

Sometimes, if no one phones for a few days and I've

used up all my old material, I'm forced to make something up. I might write that some guy had said he'd seen a flying saucer, and everyone thought he was mentally ill. I might write about how he's in torment and has no one to unburden himself to, and has finally found me at the newspaper. I might talk about his angst, as if he's a philosopher. After all, he has seen a flying saucer, and no one believes him. If you saw an article like that, you'd think I was proud at what I'd written up. But let me tell you, since the day the hotline opened, no one has called to say they've seen a flying saucer. Because there are no such things as flying saucers. All I ever hear about are failed love affairs and marriages; young people constantly slashing their wrists; forty–something women always being abandoned; STDs; drugs; gay love…I've had it all. Huh! Sometimes, I really find it hard to believe I'm sitting in the safety of my own office with a nice, scenic calendar decorating the wall. I feel like I'm on a ride to hell in a rudderless spaceship which has run out of fuel. Who knows what ghastly thing's going to happen next?

Actually, most of them just call to have a quiet moan. One tells me her husband has gone off looking for new pleasures and has ditched her for a newer model; a man says he wants to visit prostitutes but he's afraid of catching an STD. Now he's plucked up the courage to ask me whether it's true that getting gonorrhoea is no worse than catching a cold. I could tell you a hundred such cases. And I could also tell you about a hundred others: there's a girl in her twenties who's become some man's mistress and makes her living by selling her youth, never realising what she's lost but miserable all the same. Everybody bellyaches about how exhausting and hard life is. But if you suggest they try a different way of living, they say, no. That's how life is, you work your arse off and then you go and splurge it all. Until death brings an end to your troubles. If you try and tell them that death won't necessarily solve their problems or that sometimes they bring their troubles on themselves, I guarantee that no one will believe you. So there's nothing I can say. If only to keep my job, I sit here day after day waiting for those incoming calls and for someone to tell me what trouble has just hit them. It'll always be one sort of trouble or another.

Just then I looked at the aluminium office window. It seemed like a kind of great thick book, its open pages filled with a painted black sky and the dark outlines of tower blocks in the distance. What was it trying to tell me? I could see the beacon lights on the tops of skyscrapers, tirelessly blinking like so many full stops. I suddenly felt all choked up: you couldn't ever stop time passing! What I wanted to know right now was exactly what it was that was being pushed beyond the margins of the pages of this great, cold book. What was it that we'd allowed to fall through the cracks?

Suddenly the phone rang. I hurriedly pulled myself together and flicked the incoming call switch down.

'Hello, is that Lulu? I've got something to tell you.' I heard the voice of a middle-aged woman in my left ear.

'Hang on a moment,' I said, and switched the receiver to the right ear. I always made one ear work and let the other rest. I took a mouthful of tea, and screwed the lid firmly back on my mug. Then I cleared my throat and said: 'OK, you can speak now.'

For a while there was no reply. I tried again: 'Can you start by telling me a bit about yourself?'

'Not really,' she said with a sigh, and her voice grew quieter. Then she was speaking again. I could hear her now, but it sounded like she had a salted plum in her mouth.

'Are you recording this?'

I laughed. We only had an ordinary telephone, and it had no recording function. But to reassure her, because the law was still very sensitive about certain intimate matters, I said: 'No, you can relax.'

I brought the mouthpiece nearer.

She paused, then said: 'Honestly, I'm not worried about being recorded. I've read all your articles, you know.'

'Really? What do you think of them?'

'They're very good. They always ring completely true.'

'All our stories are based on callers' true stories. But if you really don't want me to write down what you say, then I won't. It doesn't matter, I can keep it confidential.'

'Oh no, I don't want it confidential. I want you to publish every detail of it. I want everyone to know.'

'Fine,' I said. I opened my notebook, clicked down on the biro cap and waited.

'But I'd like to ask you a personal question.' She hesitated, then asked: 'Are you married?'

I knew that when people had something difficult to say, they often didn't believe that their listener would understand. So I had to encourage them. 'No,' I said. 'I'm an old maid.' I stressed the words 'old maid' and put warmth into my voice, to make her feel relaxed and lighten the atmosphere a bit. Then I added: 'But don't worry, I've got a degree in Chinese and psychology. I can guarantee that I'll understand whatever you tell me.'

'That's not what I mean. What I'm saying is, if you're not married, then don't. Getting married is just so much nonsense – the reality is it's terrible.'

'Can you say a bit more about that?'

'It can completely destroy someone.'

And then she finally got into her stride. She had been married for 18 years, and as she talked about it, her voice became clearer. She seemed to have taken the plum out of her mouth now.

'I'm 43,' she said, '20 years ago I was the belle of my college. No one would believe it from the way I look now, dowdier than a cleaner.'

I knew I didn't need to say anything, it was all just going to come out. The floodgates had opened and, even if I had wanted to, it would have been difficult to get a word in edgeways. She told me she had married a fellow student who had courted her for four years and he was the love of her life.

She had one child, now at university. At this point, I felt like saying, Well that's alright then, what's the problem? But I kept quiet.

'I completely devoted myself to my family, and never had a career of my own,' she said, adding that she had given up an opportunity to study overseas as a postgraduate so as to support her husband through his science research. She had done everything for him. I didn't say a word, and she carried on. These women almost always said the same thing and it went something like this: they had slaved away and made all those sacrifices and then, just when the husband had made it and they could enjoy his success together, a third person appeared on the scene. So I waited patiently.

She loved him so much, she said. They were in the same work unit and once she'd given blood for him at their college clinic. I wondered why. Surely he had his own blood, hadn't he? But she just repeated: 'I love him so much.'

Still I waited, knowing what was coming – a young girl would suddenly burst onto the scene.

And sure enough, that was what had happened. 'My husband, that man lying in our bed, has betrayed me,' she said.

I finally got a word in: 'Your husband's at home?'

'Yes, tonight was our farewell dinner. He's drunk. I'll go and wake him up in a bit. He's going to take everything he owns and move into his girlfriend's flat tonight. He can lie there for the moment so I finish talking to you.'

She must have moved a chair, as I heard a scraping sound. Then it grew quiet again at the other end of the phone. Wherever she was, I couldn't hear a single sound.

'I didn't want to wash our dirty linen in public. I've been covering up for him for five years and during that time he hasn't stopped nagging me for a divorce so he can be with his girlfriend openly. But I just couldn't, I love him too much. I couldn't leave him, so I've put up with it and played deaf and dumb all this time. Actually, everyone at work knows. They all talk behind my back. I've become a laughing stock.'

She gave a long sigh, then repressed it and fell silent.

I never know what to say at times like this. Maybe I should have suggested something like, 'Don't be sad, Ms Wang. Or maybe you're not Wang, let's call you Ms Li, please don't be sad. Go into the kitchen, pour yourself a nice cup of tea. Sit down, just like I'm doing. Have some tea and you'll feel better. Then take a good look at yourself. There's absolutely nothing wrong with your body, and that's the truth. Honestly, you can go on living no matter who it is that you've left. That's true of every one of us....' That's what I should have said, but I didn't, I don't know why.

I heard a suppressed sob.

'Are you crying?' I asked.

'Yes, I'm always crying,' she struggled to get the words out.

'Maybe it would do you good to have a good cry.'

'I think today will be the last time.'

'I hope so. We all have to look to the future, don't we?' And then I asked a really stupid question. 'What do you look like?'

She stopped crying. 'Everyone says I'm good-looking.'

'Large eyes, fair-skinned?' I sounded even more ridiculous.

'That's right.' She'd always been proud, she said, but marriage had heaped shame and humiliation on her. For the sake of her child or rather, to be precise, for her own sake, and to keep her family together, she'd kept calm and quiet. 'Do you know, I even begged him to stay three nights a week with me and four nights with her?'

I looked down at my shoes and studied the fine cracks in the uppers. I said how much I sympathized. It really wasn't easy to be dignified nowadays, I said. I said a bit more, I can't remember exactly what. I do wander off the point sometimes.

I looked at my watch. It was five past eight – we'd been

talking for 20 minutes. I could hear she wasn't angry any more. Her voice was firm and I could not hear tears or gulps. She sounded cool and resolute.

'You're alright now?' I asked. She didn't answer, just repeated once more: 'You don't know how much he loved me then. He swore he'd love me for ever…'

'Yes, well, nothing stays the same.' I swapped the receiver over to the left ear again. I scribbled three words down in my notes: middle-aged affair. It was like the name of an ordinary illness: as far as its symptoms were concerned, we all knew what they were, there was no point wasting time describing them. Experience told me that they always ended up getting divorced. That was what always happened. The husbands always got their own way. But a forty–something divorced woman was getting on in years, hurting and on the scrap heap. I understood them only too well. And then there were those that just felt overwhelmed with regrets.

Well, anyway, she and her husband had divorced. The court had awarded her all their property and custody of their child, she told me.

'That's excellent,' I said. 'You're quite lucky. Some people get nothing at all.'

'Oh yes, I'm lucky,' she said. 'I was the belle of my college!' And she actually laughed a little – though the sound made me feel distinctly uneasy. 'Sorry, can you hang on a moment? I must just go and call him. Maybe he'll have something to say too.' She had cheered up now. 'I'll just be a moment. It might give you something new to put in your article.'

I heard the click of the receiver being put down, and a flapping sound as she walked away. She's wearing slippers, I thought. And I heard a door opening.

Then it went completely quiet at the end of the line. I agonised over whether to put the phone down or not. How much longer should I hang on? I pictured her as she was now: skinny, sallow-faced, a stack of dull, straw-like hair over her ears. Hands all wrinkled and coarsened by the washing powder. But you could still see from her large eyes how attractive she must have been as a young woman, even though now she was hollow-eyed with misery.

I pressed my ear to the receiver. If it had been morning, I should have been able to hear the odd twitter from a bird, or the flap of a wing. And at this time of night, there should have been the sound of a TV, the financial news or some sports event, or an advertising jingle. But there was absolutely nothing – just deathly silence.

I closed my notebook, clicked my biro off, then on again. I began to fiddle with it. The barrel was shaped like an hypodermic needle (a reader who worked in a hospital had given it to me). I held it between two fingers as if I was going to give someone a shot and started jabbing it into the table top.

One jab, two jabs… I had absolutely no idea what to do next. The sharp point of the biro gouged pits in the desk top. Then I heard two distant yells. I thought, she's shouting at that fickle, drunken husband of hers to get up, though I couldn't be quite sure that that was what it was. It sounded muffled. Maybe the sound had come in through her window – an adult calling a child in to dinner, perhaps. I thought, I should be somewhere else too just now. I should be at home with my imaginary husband and children eating dinner. Or strolling along a beach somewhere in the South. I should not be witnessing so much human misery. I thought of the ocean and the pure, balmy sky in the office calendar. I thought of astronauts. Chen had been dressed just like one today! What was he doing now? Making love to his girlfriend?

Two minutes later, I heard footsteps approaching. Someone picked up the receiver.

'Hello!' It was her.

'Hello. What's happened?' I said quickly. 'Does your husband want to talk to me?'

'I'm very sorry, he says he doesn't want to say anything.

He's died.'

I gasped. 'You mean, you're pretending he's dead, so he can't hurt you any more?'

'No, I killed him,' she said calmly.

'You can't have!'

'Yes, I have! Just this minute. Didn't you hear?'

My mouth felt dry and there was a lump in my throat, as if a piece of sausage had stuck in it. I could see the curved mouthpiece of the headset trembling under my nose. I couldn't get a word out.

'Don't you believe me? Listen, this is a vegetable knife and here's a fruit knife, listen to it...'

There was a grating sound in my ears. My teeth began to chatter. I didn't dare believe she was telling the truth. Any moment now, I thought, she's going to tell me it's a joke, she just wanted to scare me because I tell too many stories in my column about shameful things and no one ever gets the punishment they deserve. She's just about to say sorry. I so wanted to hear her laugh and say, 'It was a joke.' But her voice was hard and cold, and deadly serious:

'He deserved everything he got,' she said. 'I put up with it for all those years. My whole life's been destroyed. I've had enough! He just did what he pleased. He swore that he would love me forever, till death parted us. He swore.'

By the time I was able to speak again, she had put the phone down.

All I could hear was the dialing pips.

The sound of the dialing pips suddenly seemed to pour into my ear, until my head was full of them. Then they were flying around the office, more and more of them, like wriggling larvae, colliding against each other, sending terrifying echoes back from every corner.

I sprang up from the revolving chair, shouting some name or other and nearly breaking the phone cable. I was such an idiot. If she'd really done it, I should have been able to stop it... I paced up and down, perhaps just testing whether I could still make my legs work. In spite of everything, I still hadn't given up all hope. This time tomorrow she might be on the line again: 'Lulu, it was all a huge joke, and now I owe you a sincere apology.' It probably wouldn't be as long as that – she'd calm down and then she'd ring me back and say, 'Everybody needs a bit of fun, don't they?' Then she'd exclaim, 'What a life we lead, eh?!' And I would give a great sigh of relief and smile through my tears: 'I absolutely understand.'

When it comes down to it, I really am a pretty hopeless newspaper columnist.

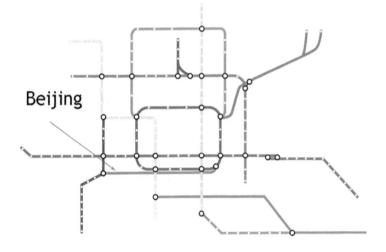
Beijing

Wheels are Round

XU ZECHEN

TRANSLATED BY ERIC ABRAHAMSEN

There was nothing in the world that Xian Mingliang couldn't dispose of with the single phrase: Wheels are round. 'Wheels are round, so just forget about it.' 'It has to be this way; wheels are round, after all.' 'All right, let's do it that way: wheels are round.' 'You just do what you please; either way wheels are still round.' 'That wheel there? Fixed it. Wheels are meant to be round.'

No need for further examples. He never stopped saying 'Wheels are round'; it was his catchphrase, the way some people never speak without first uttering a drawn-out 'Uhhhh...': usually unnecessary, often quite meaningless. Wheels. Wheels. Wheels wheels wheels. Xian Mingliang was a driver, you see.

He was already a driver when I met him, as a boy growing up in Jiangsu Province. Back then most of the men on Flower Street were either in trucking or shipping, including those who had married into the neighbourhood. When he was twenty-four he married in from Heding down-river, becoming the live-in son-in-law of the boat-boss, Huang Zengbao. Huang's daughter had been married before and had a two-year-old girl, but her husband had died while working on Huang's boat. It was a bizarre death. He'd been standing in the prow of the boat, smoking. Huang had called him below deck to eat. He'd turned his head, and then just toppled into the water like a wooden post. When they dredged him up he was cold. That husband had married into the family too. Huang had been good to him, and had planned to leave him the boat when he himself was ready to throw in the towel. But fate said otherwise: the 85-kilo brute just turned his head and died, with no room for discussion. Huang only had a daughter, and he was determined to bring in a son-in-law to carry on the family business and take over the boat that Huang had worked his whole life – he couldn't abide the thought of leaving it to someone who wasn't kin. Xian Mingliang had come to Flower Street to be a trucker, and he followed the old driver Chen Zigui everywhere he went. On long hauls he would drive and let Chen Zigui nap, slumped over in the passenger seat. He loved the feeling of operating those big Liberation-brand trucks all by himself.

When he wasn't behind the wheel Xian Mingliang seemed to deflate, and went around hands in pockets like a morose idler. All year round he wore the same style of black slacks – loose in the rear, suddenly narrowing at the calf – and let them ride low on his hips. Every time I saw him I felt they were about to fall down, and wanted to hike them up. He would greet absolutely everyone on Flower Street, and ask each kid the same question: 'Hey, little guy, did you know that wheels are round?' He was addicted to these tedious little games. If the kid knew, he would give him a piece of candy. If the kid didn't know, he'd give him the piece of candy anyway. That day on Flower Street, as he was playing with Huang's two-year-old granddaughter, holding out a piece of candy and asking if wheels were flat or round, a fortune teller arrived from the east.

In those days plenty of fortune tellers roamed from town to town making money – they said the blind ones had true vision. But the fortune teller that day wasn't blind. He couldn't be: besides making unprompted predictions he could also read bones, faces and palms. A crowd immediately gathered from all around – Flower Street was home to plenty of industrious folk, but even more idlers. As a demonstration of his abilities the fortune teller tugged his goatee (the facial hair favoured by nearly all fortune tellers), and read the faces of a few people picked out of the crowd. Meng Wanwan had a mealy face, he probably sold rice. Lan with the pockmarks – though his face was a wreck, his gaze was calm and a little weak: he was probably a tofu maker. Ma Banye had a fierce look, like he knew how to use his fists: he was sure to be a butcher. Dan Feng... He looked Dan Feng over, and considered his words for a long time before speaking. She would eventually find a man she could rely on. He could see at a glance that her trade involved opening her door to men at midnight.

Many on Flower Street had traveled extensively and knew that fortune tellers often had no skills at all. They simply made certain inquiries through certain channels ahead of time, and then used that knowledge to deceive their listeners. Once they'd gained some trust they commenced spinning yarns, blathering at will, and the money came rolling in. Someone pointed at Xian Mingliang and told the fortune teller to read him – he came from Heding, and they reckoned the fortune teller couldn't have done his homework that thoroughly.

The fortune teller took two turns around Xian Mingliang and Huang's granddaughter, then tugged his goatee and said: 'Something's not right here. This young man is plainly unmarried, and yet this girl is his daughter... though not by birth. This connection is clouded to me.'

Everyone laughed, and began to disperse. Xian Mingliang? Connected to Huang's family? What a lark. They'd caught him out after all. At that moment Huang's daughter stepped outside to throw out the laundry water, and the fortune teller suddenly pointed at her, saying: 'Those two are a couple!'

Everyone laughed all the harder, and said to Xian Mingliang: 'Why don't you help your wife throw out the water?'

The blush on Xian Mingliang's face spread all the way down to his navel but, laughing weakly, he said in his deflated way: 'I'll help her, if she agrees to be my wife. You can't tell me wheels aren't round.'

'Do you see? They will be husband and wife!' The fortune teller slung his bundle on his back and prepared to move on. 'If they're not together by the next time I pass through, you can dig out my eyes and fry them like quail eggs.'

The fortune teller arrived again three months later. Ten days before that, Xian Mingliang had moved in with the Huang family. It was because of the fortune, too. After Huang had come in from the river and heard what happened, he called Xian Mingliang in and they'd settled things on the spot. Xian Mingliang's only family was a stepfather in Heding, so he was able to make this momentous decision on his own. So what if he was marrying into his wife's family, instead of bringing a wife into his own? He was still a man, and now a father, too. The fortune teller did a spanking business that time. He held court in a tavern by the canal docks, and people came from Flower Street, East Street, West Street and South Street, cash in hand, wanting their fortunes told. My own grandfather had his face read that time, and learned that his visage bespoke great fortune: a great talent would be born among his children's children. I had just started elementary school then, and my grades really were quite good. My grandfather asked if I would attend university. He won't stop there! said the fortune teller. My grandfather was beside himself. The price was one hundred and fifty yuan: he gave two hundred.

A few years later I moved to Beijing, though not to attend college as the fortune teller had predicted. In my junior year of high school, when I was seventeen, I withdrew from school because of weak nerves. I couldn't concentrate on my books, couldn't sleep, and all day long my head felt like it was trapped in the cursed circlet they used to control the Monkey King[5]. If I'd stayed in school, I would have gone mad. All my classmates were knuckling down, trying to edge their way through the door, while I wandered through the schoolyard like a lost spirit, an outsider, a nervous wreck. One day I found a secluded place and broke down and cried, then returned to my dorm, collected my things, and went home. I told my family I'd rather die than continue my studies. I was done. My father couldn't understand how a perfectly ordinary-looking head had gone so wrong. All right then, he said, it's idleness you're after, right? Go with your uncle to Beijing and help him with his work. Earn yourself a little money, and give that strange head of yours a rest. So I followed Hong Sanwan to Beijing, and settled down in a one-storey house in the western suburbs of Haidian District. We really were out west – it wasn't all that different from being in the countryside. When we weren't in the city itself, the only way I could see it was by climbing onto the roof and looking east: Beijing was a patch of tropical rainforest, made up of endless tall buildings and the glow of neon lights.

The work I did consisted specifically of pasting little advertisements everywhere. I did it for my uncle Hong Sanwan, who made and sold fake IDs. Baolai and I were responsible for advertising his services by disseminating his phone number as widely as possible throughout the city. Baolai was in his early twenties and had been doing this a while; we slept in the same room, in bunk beds. There was another set of bunk beds in the room, where Xingjian and Miluo slept. They pasted advertisements for a different maker

5. The magical headband given to the monk Xuabzang, by Guanyin as a gift from the Bhudha, to help keep Sun Wukong (aka the Monkey King) under control. According to the epic tale, *Journey to the West*, once tricked into putting it on Sun Wukong could never take it off; Xuabzang was told that with a special chant, the band would tighten and cause unbearable pain to the monkey's head.

of fake IDs, named Chen Xingduo, and were both a little older than me. Now I'll tell you about Xian Mingliang.

'Yup, wheels can only be round, goddamn it.'

I heard a voice speak those words, and after all those years my ears still twitched. At the time I was eating dinner with Baolai at a donkey-meat eatery near where we lived. No one else would ever say anything like that – even the tone of voice sounded deflated. I turned to see Xian Mingliang sitting at another table together with a fat man with black, oily hands. Xian Mingliang was sporting a '7-3' parted hairdo, and wearing jeans instead of his old black slacks. The cuffs of his jeans were frayed at the back from being stepped on, and I guessed he still wore them low on his hips. The right side of his mouth twisted up in a grin – he appeared to have drunk too much beer. As he propped his left leg up on a stool he caught sight of me and Baolai. 'Oh, you two!' He stood up and approached us.

The fat man with the oily hands said: 'So, Mingliang, are we agreed?'

Xian Mingliang flapped a hand and said, 'I said wheels are round, didn't I? You've got to treat my two young friends here to dinner.'

'No problem.'

Xian Mingliang wanted a job in the fat man's car repair garage, and after four bottles of beer, six donkey-meat sandwiches, and three plates of garlic cucumbers they'd come to an agreement. Xian Mingliang was a skilled worker, and wasn't asking much. Earlier, when he first arrived in Beijing, he'd worked for a maker of fake IDs, and his specialty was making fake driver's licences, but he'd only made forty of them when his boss had been caught. That was the thing about this line of work – you could go in at any time. Lucky for Xian Mingliang he was a fast runner, otherwise he probably would have gone in too. He'd gone hungry for two days before finding this garage boss.

Before coming to Beijing he'd been in jail four years.

He'd run someone over with his truck. After he got married, Huang had insisted that he switch professions. After two years of apprenticeship he'd be able to run his own boat. Then Huang could finally retire and dandle his granddaughter on his knee. A grandson would be even better – he was counting on Xian Mingliang. But Xian Mingliang wouldn't listen: the only way in which he disobeyed Huang. The people on Flower Street praised Xian Mingliang, saying even a natural-born son wouldn't be so accommodating, and Huang had done well. But he refused to change his profession, because he'd wanted to be a driver ever since he was small. When he didn't have a car he'd ride a bike or drive a tractor, and would help people run their tractor-barrows for free. Later he decided to follow Chen Zigui, and finally became a driver - now he could tell everyone he saw that wheels were round.'

'I can't be bothered to argue with them,' he said with a smile when questioned about his docility. 'I just do what they say. They're not asking me to commit murder or arson; why should I worry about it? I'm fine so long as I can drive my truck – wheels are round, don't you know?'

His married life was happy, or at least it looked that way. He was very good to his abruptly-acquired two-year-old daughter, and would bring her back nice things to eat from his long hauls. The girl called him 'Papa' as though he were her real father. But just when everyone had started thinking of him as a Flower Street native, something happened.

He never thought the court should have ruled on the accident the way it did. Before he'd died the poor man really had begged him: 'My friend, I'm begging you to end it. I've got no desire to live at all. Come on, friend, I'll thank you even after I'm dead.' That struck Xian Mingliang as macabre, and the man had tried again: 'Friend, just back the truck up, my gratitude will know no bounds.' Xian Mingliang thought it couldn't be a great sin to grant a dying man his last wish, so he got back in the truck, his knees knocking, put it in reverse, and heard the man's final cry of thanks.

It was something that could only have happened at night. Given his skill as a driver, it also had to be at a fork in the road, and when he'd been drinking. He'd really pushed the boat out that day. At dusk, as he passed through the town of Tianchang in Anhui Province, the breeze had carried a sweet scent into the cab of his truck. It was a beautiful time of evening, and his truck seemed to fly. The colours of dusk rose up from the earth like drops of ink soaking up through paper, and the whole world sunk into black and grey. 'There's nothing so relaxing as driving at this time of day.' Even now Xian Mingliang thinks fondly of that evening. 'Then I got to the fork. Why must wheels be round?' His face begins to change; his lips tremble. Then it was truly dark. A bicycle hurtled out of the right-hand fork, and *bang* – by the time he'd braked to a halt, he'd gone right over it.

Xian Mingliang got out of his truck and heard someone crying out; he knew immediately he'd been in what they call an accident. He'd never in his life imagined he'd have an accident. Five metres behind the truck a man was lying next to his bicycle; both were misshapen. The bike's rear wheel was still spinning, with difficulty. The man spoke, agonizingly: 'Put me out of my misery.'

'I'll take you to the hospital,' said Xian Mingliang, shaking from head to toe.

'No, just kill me...'

Xian Mingliang thought he'd misheard. He steeled himself and approached the man. He was disabled, there was a wooden crutch nearby – it was hard to imagine how he'd ever managed to get on the bicycle. But now he was paralyzed, the truck had crushed both his thighs.

'I'll take you to the hospital.'

'No. Look at me.' He spoke haltingly. Though he wanted to die, he could hardly stand the pain. 'I waited for you at this fork for a long time. Just back up the truck, you'll be doing me a favour.' Then he began to beg.

Xian Mingliang, who must have been scared out of his

wits, agreed. 'He was asking me for help, I had to do it. As I backed up my whole body shook, from inside out, and I was covered in cold sweat – even my fingernails and toenails were sweating. Truly, you have to believe me: wheels are round, no matter what. I backed the truck up five metres, six metres, seven metres, and I heard a great cry, a sort of cry of joy. I kept backing up until the front wheels crossed over as well. I didn't know why he insisted on dying, but he wanted it so badly I had to help. Then I stopped the truck and sat by the roadside, completely soaked in sweat, waiting for the next car to come by. Ten minutes later a motorcycle appeared and I gave the driver ten yuan and told him: "Do me a favour, brother. Find a phone and call the police, tell them I'm waiting for them here."'

He told them everything, but the blue hats didn't believe him – they believed him even less when they found he'd been drinking. It was hopeless; they would do what they needed to do. However you looked at it, he'd run someone over. In court they asked him: 'Do you confess?'

He said, 'You won't believe me, so I guess I have to confess. Wheels are round.'

'What did you say?' they asked.

'I said wheels are round. That's for sure.'

'He's mad,' they said. 'Put him away!'

After he'd done four of his five years they let him out for good behaviour. He couldn't say whether his behaviour was good or not; he just did whatever they told him and spent the rest of the time napping against the wall. When he was awake he imagined his truck, from the whole to its parts and back to its whole again, mulling endlessly over every piece. In the last year he was given the opportunity to look after the upkeep of the prison vehicles; that was when he was happiest. In order to spend as much time as possible with the vehicles he would break a little something here even as he fixed a little something there; that way he could spend all his time going from vehicle to vehicle, as though it were a regular job. When he had no cars or trucks to fix he could still enjoy fixing wheelbarrows. When he got out, the prison officials praised him: He's a handy fellow.

When he returned to Flower Street he found that things had changed – there was now a one-year-old infant boy in the family. He could have understood if the little guy were three or four, but he was only one: it was a surprise. But when you got right down to it, wheels were still round, and there was nothing that couldn't be made sense of – if there was something you couldn't make sense of, it was because you didn't want to make sense of it. Xian Mingliang didn't want to, but of course he understood. Huang was smoking silently with a hired boathand in the other room. Huang's daughter sat across from Xian Mingliang, holding her yearling son, and said:

'If you don't want to accept this son, we can get divorced.'

Xian Mingliang rubbed his bald head. 'Do you want me to accept him, or do you want to get divorced?'

'It's up to you.'

'That means you want a divorce.' He stood up, walked into the yard, and called into the other room, 'I'm leaving, you can take my place.'

The smoking boathand coughed once, an expression of heartfelt gratitude, and tossed his unneeded dagger on the ground.

Baolai and I met Xian Mingliang in a donkey-meat eatery. After the accident and his time in jail Xian Mingliang couldn't find any work as a driver back home – no one would have him. Even Chen Zigui's appeals on his behalf did no good. There were superstitions in that line of work: you couldn't drive over clothing in the road, and you had to steer around dead cats and dogs too: they were unlucky. Getting into an accident that resulted in loss of life was least auspicious of all. I examined Xian Mingliang's new look: he'd exchanged his shaven head for a parting, but clearly his hair was the only thing he'd spent any time on. He'd let his hair grow long just so that he could get a look at himself in the mirror when he brushed it in the morning. A buddy in jail had told him that: you've got to look at yourself in the mirror every day, you've got to think about what you need. You can't just muddle through the days.

'So, Mingliang,' asked Baolai. 'Do you know what you need?'

'If I did, I'd shave my head again and quit looking in the mirror.'

'You need wheels to be round,' I said.

'My ass,' said Xian Mingliang. 'Don't you know wheels are *already* round?'

I wasn't sure if I knew or not. Just saying 'wheels are round' didn't mean I knew it for a fact.

Xian Mingliang had nowhere to sleep that night and wanted to stay with us. That was fine with me, I could give him my bed and squeeze in with Baolai. Baolai was fat; I was skinny. I wasn't more than ninety kilos soaking wet.

We had too much beer. Just before dawn Xian Mingliang woke with a bursting bladder, and as he headed for the bathroom he saw Baolai and me sitting on the top bunk like wise men on the mountaintop. Not only that, Xingjian and Miluo were lying awake as well. 'What are you all doing?' he asked. 'Mass qiqong?[6]'

'We can't sleep,' I said.

'Someone's setting off fireworks!' said Xingjian, turning over.

'Fireworks? Little punk! If my snoring is annoying you just wake me up; wheels are round, right? Anyway, the sun's almost up,' he said, getting dressed. 'I'm going out for a stroll,

6. Qigong or Chi Kung (pronounced 'chee-gung') is a practice of aligning breath, movement, and awareness for exercise, healing, and meditation, the purpose being to cultivate and balance *qi* ('chi') or what has been translated as 'intrinsic life energy'.

you can go back to sleep.'

'The sun's almost up,' said Baolai. 'No one's sleeping.'

'Whatever. Just don't say I interrupted your sweet dreams.'

By that point we really didn't care if we slept or not. We mostly pasted our advertisements at night. We often didn't get to bed until sunup, and we'd only knocked off early the night before because Xian Mingliang was visiting. He came back from the toilet and told us that we all ought to learn to snore, the louder the better. He'd learned it on the inside. If you couldn't do it, then forget about sleeping at night – everyone snored like it was a competition, each one louder than the next. Xian Mingliang's snores were out of all proportion to his physique – he ought to have been fifty kilos fatter. 'Do your worst,' he said to us.

Despite that, he went to sleep on the roof the next night. He arranged himself on four chairs under the canopy of the sky, and the next morning awoke with his head soaked in dew. He'd expected to live at the mechanic's garage, but there wasn't room and the stink of petrol was too strong anyway. With the door open the boss would worry about burglars, but with it closed he'd be fumigated. He liked cars, but not enough to be fumigated. But he couldn't sleep long-term in the open air either – the wind changed to come from the north and Beijing cooled down. It was breezy on the roof. The roof was used for a lot of things: we played a card game called Ace of Spades up there. Whoever drew the Ace of Spades was the enemy of the other three. You had to keep that close to your chest. If they knew you had it they would gang up to destroy you, and if you were destroyed you had to treat everyone to beer and kebabs. Xian Mingliang would come up on the roof when business was slow in the garage and play Ace of Spades with us. It used to be Baolai who always drew the ace, but now Xian Mingliang drew it hand after hand, and hand after hand was attacked by the rest of us. Empty bottles from all the beer he treated us to were lined up in ranks along the wall. The roof had another important use: it was where we climbed up to look at Beijing.

A couple of weeks later Xian Mingliang got his first salary advance, and rented a little room in the alley to the left of us. The first day he was too late to buy a sleeping mat, and he spent that night on the bare mattress. He lived simply, and enjoyed his work in the garage. He had a hobby, which was to gather together unused car parts – he said eventually he'd have enough to make his own car. Normally such parts could be sold for scrap, and even the small ones brought in a little cash sometimes. His fat boss bemoaned the loss and said: 'You can take those away, but when customers come in the future you've got to use the best parts on their cars; you've got to earn it back double.'

'So long as they follow my suggestions,' said Xian Mingliang.

While I was out jogging I'd often pass by his room. The doctor had told me that the best cure for weak nerves was jogging, which would gradually restore flexibility to flaccid nerves, and once they resembled elastic bands fresh from the factory, you were cured. So now I jogged every day, imagining my head to be full of elastic bands that grew gradually tighter the more I ran, and I'd stop at his room any time he was home. The scrap metal heaped in the corner really was scrap, pitch-black and filthy – given my weak nerves I lacked the imagination to see that heap becoming a shiny new car. But he had a detailed blueprint in his head, and knew precisely where each piece of wrecked metal would go.

'Behold, comrades, our mighty capital!' After a game of Ace of Spades, Miluo would gesture south-eastwards like a great leader, and that lyric right arm seemed to extend farther and farther until it became a bird that flew right over Beijing. We four young men (counting me, who'd never graduated from high school) viewed this vast and bustling capital with boundless expectation. Everyone in the whole country knew this place was full of money, you only had to bend down and pick it up; everyone in the whole country also knew that opportunity here was like birdshit – while you weren't looking it would spatter on your head and make you rich. From what I'd seen, however, there were fewer and fewer birds in Beijing; the place used to be full of sparrows and crows but you hardly ever saw them now. They said it was because the glass in the skyscrapers dazzled them and led them to smash against the walls. There were still some parrots, thrushes, and magpies but they were mostly in cages; you couldn't expect them to fly up and shit opportunity on you. In the end we might be left with a single bird in the sky – Miluo's lyric right hand, which no matter what, would never shit on you. But that couldn't disturb the sweet dreams of all the young people rushing towards Beijing.

We gazed out from our heights. As the westering sun slowly sank, the twilight rose up from the streets that lay like narrow ravines between the buildings, mixing with the exhaust from uncountable cars and the sour breath of the exhausted office workers heading home. We gazed on Beijing together.

Xingjian said: 'If I could just earn enough, I'd buy an apartment, marry a wife nine years older than me, and spend my days lying in bed. A twenty-eight-year-old woman... Just thinking about it gets me excited!'

Miluo said: 'If I had money I'd have a house and a wife, of course. Also I'd take a taxi every time I left the house, I'd take a taxi to the toilet! And I'd find a bunch of people, like you guys, to go around in the middle of the night and paste advertisements for me. I'd have more money than fucking Chen Xingduo! Too cheap to buy a car? I told you I've got no sense of direction, the Third Ring Road's enough to make me dizzy. I could set out for Fangshan and end up in Pinggu.'

Baolai said: 'I'd own a bar, with the most expensive wallpaper, and I'd tell everyone who drank there to write whatever they wanted to on the walls.'

It was my turn. I didn't actually know what I wanted.

Maybe I should have let my hair grow and looked at myself in the mirror each morning.

'Just say you had 500,000, man.'

500,000 – that must be what they meant by an 'astronomical figure'. I had no idea how I would spend it. Would I build a new house where my sixty-year-old grandma and grandpa could live out their years? Buy my dad a truckload of point-eight Zhongnanhai cigarettes? Exchange my mother's rotten teeth for a set of the best ceramic dentures, and then dye each one of her prematurely white hairs back to black? As for myself, if anyone could cure my weak nerves I'd give them the rest of the money.

'Fucking weak!' said Xingjian and Miluo. 'Your turn, Mingliang.'

We all looked at him. He hiked up his jeans (at last I'd seen him hike up his trousers) and wiped his mouth – articulating his great ideal was a hazardous thing. Perhaps what he needed at that moment was a mirror. But he looked out over Beijing's distant rolling skyline, his gaze soaring like Miluo's right hand, then sliding on down to rest on a highway at the other end of the town.

'I'd like a car,' he said, dropping into his chair and propping one leg on the other. 'I'd find some empty road and drive. Just keep driving. Wheels are round, you know.'

It was a pretty disappointing ideal. Just driving around in some wrecked car – what was the point of driving?

One evening Xian Mingliang visited our room and asked us to help him move. His voice was nasal, sounding as though it were coming from Beijing's distant eastern suburbs. His nose dripped a clear liquid and his eyes were red. His room was so packed with spare parts that he'd had to move his bed just outside the door, and after sleeping there two nights he'd gotten a bad cold. We could hardly imagine how he could sleep on such chilly nights, a skyful of stars hanging over him. I felt his blanket – it seemed like a firm squeeze would wring water out of it. The five of us could only worm our way into the six-metre-square room through cracks and gaps. The scrap metal really was just junk, though he'd arranged it convincingly (we didn't understand a thing, of course, but getting all those bits and bobs in one place had to count for something) – filthy and black, it wasn't very confidence-inspiring. We nearly exhausted ourselves moving the whole pile out under the eaves, then helping him bring his bed and an old table back inside. These two jobs done, we put up a little shack under the eaves, to cover the car guts – Xian Mingliang didn't want them exposed to wind and sun and rain. Xian Mingliang knew exactly what to do with this incomprehensible pile. 'Just wait,' he said. 'When it's done I'll take you out for a spin; you can't tell me wheels aren't round.'

A week later he called us over again – the car guts were gradually taking shape, and needed to be moved to the garage, where they'd eventually be joined up with a chassis and wheels. We borrowed a bicycle cart from the old grocer next door and made two creaking, straining trips. The fat boss wasn't happy to have so many idle young men hanging around his garage, but Xian Mingliang passed him a cigarette and explained we were all buddies from the same street, and we were all clean. It was like we were there to steal something. 'What the fuck *is* this?' asked Xingjian.

In the garage I saw a half-made car body welded together out of rusty metal sheeting, little droplets of metal stuck to the seams. There were wheels, too, four of them, apparently of different sizes. Xian Mingliang said he hadn't been able to find four identical wheels, and it was a miracle that he'd found two matching pairs. I'd once thought that, if he couldn't find four, he could just start by making a three-wheeled car. A three-wheeled car is still a car, and wheels are round. I couldn't imagine how a three-wheeler would look driving along Beijing's thoroughfares – perhaps like Neanderthals appearing on our Flower Street?

After that, Xian Mingliang had good news for us each

time he came to the roof to play Ace of Spades: 'Almost there!' We were waiting for the day when he drove himself over. And one weekend, after Xian Mingliang got off work, he really did drive over. Scared the crap out of us. I can say with confidence that no more than a handful of human beings have ever laid eyes on a car like that one: it was a monster. Its skin was still rusted sheeting – I mean not a speck of paint – that was all he could afford. Never mind that, there wasn't even enough to go around: he'd been obliged to make a convertible. The rust-spotted convertible was covered in bright patches where he'd ground the metal droplets from the welding seams. Only those polished patches gleamed under the sun. Leaving aside the wretched seating, scavenged from other people's cast-offs, the major problem seemed to be that the front wheels were smaller than the back wheels, and the whole car seemed to lunge forward angrily.

'Get in!' said Xian Mingliang. 'These are the roundest wheels you've seen!'

We got in and took a turn through the local alleys – it would be dangerous to go on the main roads without a licence plate. It wasn't too strange, same as being in any other car, apart from the way it tilted forward: I had to brace my feet against the legs of the seat in front to keep from sliding forward. That was fixable: just raise the seat. The licence plate could also be resolved. A word from me and Hong Sanwan would make a fake one, and it wouldn't cost more than a few bottles of beer. Two days later everything was sorted, and we decided to try the main roads.

It had horsepower, just like Xian Mingliang said. It made a lot of noise, but it certainly moved. The low front and high back made it seem like it was raring to go, like it couldn't be stopped. He'd used the best materials he could find in the rubbish on this car. There weren't many cars out at night in the countryside beyond the suburbs, and they all drove fast, but we overtook them all. We howled as we passed each one – the cold wind swept over the open car, and we had to do something to keep ourselves warm. The drivers we passed could only gaze in despair at our fake licence plate. Then, somewhere in Mentougou District, the engine stalled, and we were stranded in the wilds.

Xingjian and the others got out and opened up the last two bottles of beer while I held the light for Xian Mingliang as he worked out what went wrong. As the beer cooled off we started feeling the chill ourselves. Xian Mingliang fiddled with every part he could think of, but the car remained a pile of metal, even colder than we were. Soon our main priority was getting warm, so Xian Mingliang gave up and set us collecting dry grass, branches and bricks from the side of the road. He drew a little gas from the tank and lit the branches, and we baked the bricks and rocks. Around the time that both we and the rocks started to warm up he suddenly slapped his forehead, reached behind the steering wheel (formerly Honda), and the engine turned over.

'Goddamn it!' He yelled. 'Wheels are round!'

He showed us how to wrap the hot rocks in newspaper and hold them in our laps to keep warm – one of the survival tactics he'd learned as a truck driver. Restored to roaring life, the car leaped forward as if desperate to get out of there.

'Let's name this thing!' said Baolai.

Xingjian said: 'Iron Horse!'

Miluo said: 'Land Tiger!'

I said: 'Stallion!'

"Stallion' it is,' said Xian Mingliang. 'Wheels are round!'

We hadn't anticipated the influence 'Stallion' would have: within ten days it was the mascot of the boss' garage. Just parked outside it was a constant advertisement, less a car than a piece of rough-hewn art. What skills this mechanic must have, to create such a powerful, mad-looking machine out of abandoned parts! The fat boss was happy at first, but less happy later: Xian Mingliang often left the car parked in his own alley, and when customers who'd come to the garage to gawk – and maybe buy some spare parts and get some repairs done – saw nothing outside, they simply sped away.

'You've got to leave that car outside the garage,' said the boss.

'I suppose I could,' said Xian Mingliang. 'But I'm worried someone will mess with it, and that fake licence plate isn't going to hold up.'

'You've got to.'

'All right, I will. I can't help wheels being round.'

The garage was about a twenty-minute walk from where Xian Mingliang lived, a walk Xian Mingliang never minded before, but now that he had the Stallion it seemed awfully far. Worse than that was, any time it started to rain or blow he had to run over and put a raincoat on it. Then he had to come back. He wanted to buy some car sheeting and cover it up at the end of each work day – the money could come out of his salary. The boss glared at him: what was the difference between covering it up and just driving it away? If he wanted to cover it, he could only cover the steering wheel and dashboard. That was infuriating, but Xian Mingliang had no choice – wherever the Stallion was it had to be protected from wind and rain; he had to go and swaddle it.

But that wasn't the end of the issue: some meddling bastard came to the boss wanting to buy it. He thought it was cool, it had personality: the perfect combination of artistry and practicality. 'Sure, it's cool,' the guy said. 'But it's the roughness I like. I'll give you a figure.' He wiggled some fingers, wiggling the fat boss right out of his gourd. He revealed this figure to no one, but it was enough to buy a brand new Toyota. The guy added that scrap metal by itself was worthless, but once made into something like this...

The boss brought Xian Mingliang to the donkey-meat place and ordered four bottles of beer, four donkey-meat sandwiches, and a plate of five-spice donkey meat. There's something we've got to discuss, he said. Xian Mingliang drank the beer and ate the meat: 'What's on your mind? Either way wheels are round.'

'Just leave the car outside the garage, I'll give you a raise.'

'No need, I made it in my spare time.'

'I'll triple your salary,' said the boss, opening the fourth bottle of beer, 'and the car belongs to the garage.'

'It'll be yours?'

'That's not what I'm saying. It will belong to the garage. And the garage belongs to all of us.'

'It already does belong to the garage.'

'Well just sign here, then.' The boss pulled a paper out of his trouser pocket. At the top was written: Deed of Transfer. He'd already signed under his own name.

Xian Mingliang said it was the first time in his life he'd just walked out. He stood, called for the bill, dropped thirty kuai on the table, and left. He came to our place to finish dinner. His luck was bad, he was caught out with the Ace of Spades, and had to pay for four bottles of beer. At the time we had no idea that a price had been offered for Stallion, we were just pissed at how he'd been treated: 'Our Xian Mingliang grubbed in the rubbish each night, putting it together screw by screw, and you were just going to take it away?' we wanted to say to the guy. 'Are you local government or something?'

Xingjian said: 'Listen to me, brother, keep your eye on that thing. Wheels are round, right?'

'Yup,' said Xian Mingliang. 'Wheels are round. All I wanted was a car. Even one as run-down as this: why was that so hard?'

The next day he returned, saying, 'He said I used his tools, his electricity.'

'What did you say?' we asked.

'I said I could pay him.'

The day after he came again, saying, 'He said I got a fake licence plate, that's illegal.'

'What did you say?' we asked.

'I said I could get a real one.'

'And then?'

'He said I'd already broken the law. And I've got a record, if they take me in again I'll never come out. Goddamn, wheels are round.'

The day after that he came again, saying, 'Today a police officer came to the garage and walked around the Stallion three times. He asked me where I was from, and about my family, and whether life was good in Beijing.'

'What did you say?' we asked.

'I said my stepfather died and I had no family. I said so long as I could see that car outside, I thought life in Beijing was pretty good.'

That day he played Ace of Spades with us on the roof until we couldn't see the cards in our hands. He treated us to beer, donkey-meat sandwiches and five-spice donkey meat. As the sky darkened we couldn't see his expression, and couldn't be bothered to look too closely; we all had good hands, and were fidgeting in our haste to catch the Ace. The five-spice donkey meat was excellent, it included donkey heart, donkey liver, donkey lungs, donkey tripe, and so on.

A couple of days later we heard that something had happened to Xian Mingliang. Something had happened to his fat boss, too – when he was going to make a booze delivery to the Zhang family at the foot of the Fragrant Hills. Xian Mingliang asked if he could drive the Stallion there. He drove fast – it was the Stallion, after all – and as he was making a left turn the front left tyre fell off. His boss, sitting in the passenger seat, flew out of the car then turned over a few times with it. The remaining three differently-sized wheels spun against the evening sky. The boss went headfirst into a tree trunk and pushed his head right into his chest – it took the doctors ages to pull it out.

The four of us went to visit Xian Mingliang where he lay in the hospital with four broken ribs. His head was wrapped in an enormous bandage, and his left arm was broken. Miluo — who'd resolved never to drive a car as long as he lived — timidly asked the question we were all curious about: why hadn't the boss worn his seat belt?

'Is there a seat belt on the passenger side?' asked Xian Mingliang with some difficulty. 'I'm sure I never installed one there.'

Miluo wondered if he'd remembered wrong. When he'd sat there last time, wasn't it the seat belt Xian Mingliang had insisted he fasten?

'Did they find the wheel?' Every time he spoke, four ribs hurt.

'They did,' we said. 'It rolled into the dry grass at the roadside. Don't worry, it didn't lose its shape — it was still round.'

Shenyang

Squatting

Diao Dou

Translated by Brendan O'Kane

SUMMER IS HIGH season for criminal offenses, particularly at night.

I'm not just referring to crimes of a sexual nature.

That sexual assault is more prevalent during the summer months, and especially on summer nights, is a fact in need of little explanation. Indeed, summer nights facilitate many other forms of crime, as may also go without saying.

Brawling, for example. On summer nights, when the heat lifts a little and a light breeze blows, when outdoor barbecue stands line both sides of the street and fill the air with the aroma of roasting meat, even people who have already eaten dinner will take the chance to slip away from their stifling homes and sit out on the benches by the barbecue stands, drinking beer and husking boiled peanuts or brined flatbeans, nibbling at skewers of roast chicken or slices of kidney or grilled fish, gossiping with friends, playing drinking games, growing louder and rowdier as the night wears on. The combination of strangers in close quarters, alcohol fanning the flames, and a conversational milieu consisting largely of idle chatter, boasts, and swagger is ripe for disagreements, for conflict, for violence, for incidents leading to injury or even grievous bodily harm.

Or robbery. It is considerably harder to rob someone's person in the winter, when layers of heavy clothing pile up so thickly that no sooner has one shoved the victim into a narrow alleyway or a grove of trees or a tight corner, than one has to rifle through a dozen pockets in different layers of clothes – tissues in this pocket, handkerchief in that one, nothing at all in that one over there – and there's no guarantee one will even find the money before a patrolman comes running. Much more straightforward in the summer, when people only have a couple of places to store things on their person and the pickings are easier by far.

Breaking and entering likewise. Doors and windows are shut tight in the wintertime but left quite agape in the summer. Many individuals who might be merely satisfying their own vulgar curiosity by peeking through other people's windows will find, after discovering the ease of egress and the convenient placement of mobile phones on tables and wallets in handbags, that one thing simply leads to another, a problem of morality becoming a problem for the courts.

Or homicide. Chinese people don't possess guns, or at any rate have generally not got access to them, so most murder weapons are improvised – clubs, hammers, axes, screwdrivers and whatnot. The padded jackets and insulated hats of winter wrap their wearers so thickly that an attacker using insufficient or improperly applied force will find that even with a perfectly timed attack, these improvised weapons will let them down almost every time. They may manage to tear a hole in the victim's cotton-stuffed vest or down jacket, or to knock the victim's cotton or leather or woolen cap out of shape, but the victim will remain physically unharmed, possibly reeling for an instant before understanding the situation. Whereupon most people will bolt like startled rabbits – but from time to time a victim made of tougher stuff will respond by rearing up like a horse and pouncing like a tiger, and *then* there's no telling who will end up killing whom. Summer homicides are a different matter altogether, and a malefactor of sufficient strength and accuracy will be able to effect the expiration of their victim with nothing more than a single well-placed blow.

Summer is beautiful, and summer nights more beautiful still, but in our city it was a deadly beauty.

The above shouldn't be taken to reflect the primary characteristics of summer nights in our city – merely a single aspect, incidental, a footnote to a greater whole. In principle, I believe, the overall mainstream big picture situation of our city at the macro level is hardly different from Paris or Warsaw, Pyongyang or London, Tokyo or Beijing, Baghdad or Port-au-Prince, Canberra or Kabul, Sarajevo or Caracas, Addis Ababa or Buenos Aires. Not that I've been to any of these cities – but insofar as issues of public security are concerned I am confident, going by common sense, deductive reasoning, and what I've seen in books and television, that the problem of increased crime during summer months is by no means limited to the city in which I live. That it is a general phenomenon by whose very commonness we may see that conflicts will arise anywhere people are gathered, and that promoting public morality and social progress is not as simple a matter as, say, acquiring a new production line for the manufacture of televisions or refrigerators or washing machines. Far from it. The road to a better world, as the poet said, is a long and winding one. My colleagues and I therefore composed a delicately couched, politely worded, mildly phrased letter along these lines to the highest-ranking municipal administrator – not to criticize or assign blame or complain or bellyache or grumble; merely an earnest, sincere, humble, written reminder that summer was nearly upon us and, with it, peak season for crimes, and that we hoped the highest-ranking municipal administrator and the relevant departments would find the time to note the passing of the seasons and make such preparations as might be needful.

We sent the letter in the middle of April, when the air was cool and crisp.

Every year summer comes to our city a few days earlier than the year before, owing supposedly to the greenhouse effect. Meteorological authorities had already said it would be another veritable scorcher: even our far-northern city would be running into temperatures of 25 degrees Celsius or higher by the start of May, and authorities couldn't – or wouldn't, or at least couldn't honestly – say how hot it would be come July and August. Indeed, by the beginning of the May Day holiday week anyone setting foot outside was instantly inspired to change into shorts and undershirts; meanwhile air conditioners, fans, window-screens, and cool bamboo sleeping mats sold out overnight. During those first few days of the May Day holiday, all of our city's media outlets – the 'three mouthpieces' of newspapers, radio, and television – began replacing front page and prime time coverage of tourism revenues with reports on a new regulation from the municipal Counter-Criminal Crackdown Command Office, stipulating that starting after the May Day holiday week, all public buses, motorcycles, bicycles, and other human-powered vehicles would be barred from city streets between the hours of 8pm and 5am.

There was a public outcry, in response to which 'CrackCom' issued a full explanation of the new regulation.

The explanation was faithfully transmitted by all news outlets. Through a barrage of interviews, special features, opinion pieces, letters from the editor, recorded lectures, public service announcements, televised exposés, and topical artistic performances, newspapers and radio and television stations informed the masses that while the new regulation would, most certainly, result in minor public inconvenience, any honest comparison against the major public inconvenience of rampant nocturnal criminality would conclude that the restrictions on the 'three categories of vehicles' were merely a small inconvenience. The brilliance of the new regulation, in other words, lay in using a minor inconvenience to the public to utterly eliminate the major inconvenience of criminal activity; in employing a minor curtailing of the public's ability to do its business in order to allow the authorities to discharge their duty of wiping out criminal elements; in engineering a beneficial trade-off between inconvenience and convenience.

The logic behind the regulation was straightforward. Having buses, motorcycles, and bicycles on the roads at night contributed to crime: some vehicles, such as buses, were sites of criminal activity; some, such as motorcycles and bicycles, were implements of crime; some, such again as motorcycles and bicycles, were targets of crime. There were pickpockets and hooligans on buses by day, but at night they ran rampant; likewise, there were daytime thefts of motorcycles and bicycles, and thieves who snatched at people's wallets, necklaces, and mobile phones from moving bicycles and motorcycles during the daytime, but under cover of night the snatching and thievery became downright brazen. If, during the dark hours from 8pm to 5am, these three categories of vehicle were barred from city streets, then the problems might be resolved, and the ability of criminal elements to commit crimes effectively restricted. Gesturing with his hands as he addressed the television cameras, a CrackCom spokesman said: 'Ladies and gentlemen, citizens of our fair city, we have every reason to believe that this summer will see a sharp drop in crime rates in our city.'

The residents of our city are understanding, law-abiding sorts – except for the criminals – and after an initial period of stunned silence the public came to appreciate the municipal government's concern, and took to the media to express its full support for CrackCom's new regulation. Public support or no, however, the new regulation undeniably gave rise to more than a few new problems – most obvious of which, and anticipated by CrackCom, was the massive inconvenience caused to the work and everyday life of people throughout the city.

The inconvenience to people who began or ended their work shifts at night may be imagined. Even for those who didn't, the inconvenience will be readily apparent. People couldn't just barricade themselves indoors talking or making love or watching TV or playing mahjong as soon as the sky began to darken. Many enjoyed taking evening strolls – but how, once outside, were these ordinary citizens to get anywhere without buses or motorcycles or bicycles or other everyday means of transport? More troublesome still: if, at 8pm, a bus or a motorcycle or a bicycle or a cargo tricycle was out on the roads, it would be compelled to stop where it was by the sight of a police car zooming by on its rounds, or by the deafening blast of sirens that signaled the beginning of the curfew. This was no problem for people who were within sight of their homes – they could simply get off and walk, or gun the throttle a couple of times and slip in under the wire – but what about those left stranded between work and home? Unable to afford taxi fare, bus passengers would have to disembark and contemplate the long road ahead of them; riders of bicycles, motorcycles, and tricycles faced the additional question of what to do with their vehicles. The regulation banned even pushing a bicycle between the hours of 8pm and 5am, since any moving motorcycles, bicycles, or even tricycles would place patrolling officers in a position of having to ascertain whether the people pushing the vehicles were thieves or the vehicles' rightful owners.

And then there were secondary issues not to be overlooked. In one instance, the sudden blast of the curfew alert startled an old lady so severely as to affect her heart. Some drivers, lacking proper respect for CrackCom's new regulation, would gleefully follow the curfew alert by leaning on their horns, resulting in a blast of urban noise pollution in excess of the regulated three minutes. A young boy on a bicycle forgot what the 8pm alert was for and kept pedaling through the streets while other cyclists throughout the city stopped in their tracks – presenting a problem for the patrolling officer who caught him, since detention or fines would be inappropriate given the boy's status as a minor. An old scrap collector pedaling back to the little shack he rented was so startled by the alert that he overturned his cargo tricycle, scattering rubbish all over the roadway and bringing the remaining legitimate traffic to a halt for fifteen minutes, infuriating the motorists on the scene. One woman chained her scooter to a sapling by the side of the street; upon returning to retrieve it in a car two hours later, she and her husband found that the scooter and the newly planted tree it had been chained to were both gone, leaving only a shallow pit.

Though by no means common, such problems could only lead to greater problems in the future if they continued to go unaddressed. After spending nights compiling a list of such cases, my colleagues and I wrote an urgent letter to the highest-ranking municipal administrator, which we passed to one of his secretaries through the secretary's wife in order to ensure prompt delivery. It was our hope that the highest-ranking municipal administrator would receive our report on recent conditions from his secretary the following morning.

(It should be noted that one of our number had attended university with the wife of one of the highest-ranking municipal administrator's secretaries, and had for some years been romantically involved with her).

My colleagues and I weren't People's Congress delegates or People's Political Consultative Committee members, nor indeed were we employees of any governmental authority. We were writers of reportage, teachers of history, players of oboes, designers of computer software, extractors of teeth, translators of foreign languages, creators of advertisements, students of calculus, researchers of pharmaceutical compounds. We'd all gone to university and taken at least undergraduate degrees, and if forced to give an account of ourselves we would shyly admit to being intellectuals. Engaged in different lines of work, living in different neighbourhoods, of different ages and genders, we shared nonetheless a common concern for the development and growth of our city, and wrote regular letters to a succession of highest-ranking municipal administrators addressing the strengths and shortcomings of our city and the strengths and shortcomings of municipal policy in the hopes that our suggestions would aid them in the performance of their duties. Our efforts were motivated not by a desire for official recognition or pecuniary reward, but by a sense of righteousness and justice, of responsibility, of social morality, and of love for our fellow man.

Our little group had its roots in a happy coincidence some years before.

While other parts of our city had prospered, the west side was at the time still a desolate swathe of brick shacks, linked together by a few secondary roads, that stared out uncomfortably at the rest of the city. Any attempt to change the fortunes of the west-side slums was bound to be an uphill battle – but, we felt, a battle well worth fighting! Leaving aside more complex issues like housing and employment for the time being, we felt that the simpler issue of transportation could be readily addressed through public transit links between the west side and the rest of the city, and that the remaining problems might not seem so insoluble once this had been accomplished. In virtually every other part of the city, even the unimportant roads were immaculately paved, bordered by gleaming sidewalks lined with emerald trees stretching as far as the eye could see, punctuated at intervals by red and green lights merrily a-twinkle. But on the west side of the city, even arterial roads like Huashan Road or Qishan Road or Buyunshan Road were little better than the dirt roads of the wild northwest: on clear days, they were covered in thick clouds of dust; on rainy days, water pooled waist-deep; and they were so pitted and rutted, rain or shine, that even any senior cadres driving over them would find their sedans being tossed to and fro like boats on a choppy sea. Not that senior cadres took these roads – their residences and offices weren't in the area. Even when municipal inspection teams visited our city from the Central Committee, and foreign guests and overseas compatriots came, saying that they wanted to see every nook and cranny of the city, nobody ever visited that part of town. But we felt that a lack of visits from officials and foreign friends shouldn't mean that the west side never got to see brighter days. A city is a single organism. Allowing one part of an organism to wither away while the rest of the organism develops might seem to have no effect in the short term – other than a possible saving in development expenditures – but if matters continued as they had been, the imbalance could potentially cause incalculable damage to the appearance, structure, and overall progress of the whole. Consider a family in which the majority of members never touch tobacco or strong drink, but one member becomes addicted to drugs. The addict's cash-flow and health problems may not initially affect the other members of the family, but as his money runs low and his health begins to fail, he becomes progressively likelier to drag all the others down with him. Seeing the condition of the west side of our city and its key roads in much the same light, we wrote down our observations in letters which we sent to the official then serving as the highest-ranking municipal administrator, humbly requesting that he consider the west side of town and its pitiful roads.

None of us had ever met any of the others at the time, I hasten to add. Each of us was perfectly unaware of the others' existence. We were making our proposals as individuals, and so naturally our letters went out separately.

The letters' common addressee was nonplussed, as you may imagine, to receive so many letters containing roughly the same content at more or less the same time. His bemusement gave way to nervousness and suspicion, and he turned the letters over to the Public Security Bureau. Someone who was with him at the time told us later that he had suspected us of being American spies or Russian special agents before deciding that we were catspaws of a political rival, or at least plants hired by a rival to stir up the waters and force him to resign. After analyzing the letters, the Public Security Bureau agreed that the evidence suggested a conspiracy. The cover story – that a group of people from disparate backgrounds had written letters for purposes other than pleading their own cases, complaining about their own mistreatment, or making personal demands – was transparently flimsy, and yet the PSB had no idea what to make of letters from authors scattered all around the city – except for the west side, where none of them lived – on the subject of roads on the west side of the city that had nothing to do with them. The more the PSB analyzed the letters, the more serious the situation grew: they raised the municipal security alert level and deployed officers on the west side of town, particularly around Huashan, Qishan, and Buyinshan Roads, while also employing every available method of detection to investigate the senders of the letters and conduct round-the-clock surveillance and tracking operations. Fortunately none of us had sent our letters anonymously, and fortunately we were all cleaner than a fresh sheet of paper and purer than water. The PSB realized soon enough that it had blown matters out of proportion, and reported to the highest-ranking municipal administrator that we posed no threat whatsoever. In its report, the PSB attributed the coincidence of our letters to the fact that we were a bunch of intellectuals who minded other people's business for fun instead of playing mahjong or going out with friends or getting massages or singing karaoke. Embarrassed at his own overreaction, and perhaps eager to create an impression of being open to good advice, the highest-ranking municipal administrator actually did take our suggestions to heart. In addition to repairing Huashan, Qishan, and Buyunshan Roads, he drafted an urban rejuvenation plan for the west side of the city with the stirring slogan of 'One Small Step in One Year, One Medium Step in Two Years, and One Big Step in Three Years.'

His successors must have heard the story, because subsequent letters were not forwarded to the PSB, and the urban rejuvenation plan ultimately did make the transition from paper to reality. Like anywhere else in this changing city of ours, the west side today is full of bright lights and all the trappings of healthy prosperity, of families living together in peace and loving kindness in the high-rises that dot the area, and citizens coexisting in amicable fraternity on the streets outside. The public order and strong governance our city enjoys today is due in no small measure to the way the west side was reunited with the rest of the city. Despite improvements, crime rates are admittedly still higher than average – especially during summer, and most especially on summer nights – but this is merely a small bump in the road, the brief darkness before the dawn. I will extend the analogy I laid out earlier: the addict's family has successfully prevailed upon him to change his ways, and he finally understands the importance of just saying 'no' – but he can hardly be expected to quit cold turkey.

But of this, no more. I still have to say how my colleagues and I found one another.

During the PSB's upsetting investigation of us, we'd had to submit evidence proving ignorance of one another, lack of organizational structure, freedom from external control, and absence of malicious intent. But there was an unexpected benefit – namely, discovering that there were others out there who shared our goals and our sensibilities. The woman who did computers and the man who did ads were the first to meet each other after the investigation wrapped up, and they promptly fell in love. Using the list of names the PSB had compiled, they contacted us one by one and brought the whole group together. From then on, acting as a loose collective of friends sharing a mutual concern for the public welfare, we resumed offering advice to the highest-ranking municipal administrators with renewed vigor and enthusiasm. We never received any response from the relevant departments, other than the investigation; nor did we come in for any praise or criticism. But we believed that many of our suggestions had been taken seriously by a succession of highest-ranking municipal administrators and the relevant departments, meaning that at least a tiny smidgen of the credit for the continued prosperity, rejuvenation, modernization, and growing cultural sophistication of our city belonged to us – or rather, to our letters.

We wrote letters beyond counting in the years that followed, and countless numbers of people joined or left our loose collective as their interests changed or their passions shifted. Throughout all of this, whether our ranks were swollen or depleted, we continued not to form a civilian organization or to even admit that we were an organization of any description. We had no name, no program, no charter, no stated goal. Every letter we sent to the highest-ranking municipal administrators of our city was a personal letter: if it was written by one person, then one person would sign; if by three people, then three people would sign; if by seven, then seven would sign. If there were disagreements on an issue, but people felt that the issue needed to be aired, then we would each write our own letters, or one faction would write a letter expressing its views and another group would write its own letter. Our members exercised the strictest self-discipline: never once did anybody attempt to seek personal gain by means of their 'public service letters.'

Never before had we seen such a rapid response!

Three days after we sent off our letter, CrackCom published a set of supplementary recommendations that rendered the new regulation instantly more humane. Firstly: the sudden three-minute siren at 8:00 was to be replaced with three snippets of classical music, each one minute long, starting at 7:50. Specifically: at 7:50 PM, there would be a minute of the Czerny études; at 7:54, a minute of the allegro from Chopin's *Les Sylphides*; at 7:59 another minute, this time of the famous Fate-knocking-at-the-door motif from

Beethoven's Fifth. In this way citizens would be reminded and given advance warning before the curfew, and instead of harsh sirens, the alerts would promote high art in a clear case of killing two birds with one stone. Secondly: the city had recruited 10,000 migrant workers on short notice, and set them working around the clock to put up simple shelters anywhere around the city there was sufficient empty space. These were to be used by cyclists as 8:00 drew near for the free storage of their motorcycles, bicycles, and cargo tricycles, to which end CrackCom and the Urban Law Enforcement Bureau had also hired, at no small expense, a crop of strapping young unemployed men – priority given to those with martial arts training – to act as nightwatchmen for the bicycles. Finally: people who were caught on buses at 8:00, or who locked their motorcycles or bikes in a shed far from home or work, would be eligible for partial reimbursement of taxi fare. Anyone who could present a taxi receipt time-stamped after 8pm, marked with the starting point, destination, and circumstances of the cab ride, and stamped with the official seal of their work unit or the residential committee where they lived, would be eligible for reimbursement of two-thirds of the fare by CrackCom. At the discretion of representatives of the person's work unit or residential committee, two-thirds of the remaining one-third of the fare could also be reimbursed, with a full report of expenses incurred in the reimbursement thereof to be presented to CrackCom by the applicable work unit or residential committee at the end of the month.

Once the new recommendations were announced, what little public resentment there had been simply evaporated, and people went happily back to their everyday work and life routines with relatively minor changes. No less happily, my colleagues and I discussed writing a letter of thanks in the form of a poem expressing our gratitude at having city fathers and mothers who cared for us more deeply than our own parents had. The person drafting the letter likened the city leaders to 'father and mother' and 'dad and mum,' and cast us and our fellow citizens as 'children' and 'sons and daughters,' a rhetorical flourish that set our little group of thin-skinned intellectuals squabbling. The war of words ended with a decision to leave the phrasing in, even though it did betray a rather serf-like mentality, if only because the government leaders' solicitous concern for their citizens really did reflect nothing so much as parental love.

We mailed our encomium with a long sigh of contentment in the knowledge that at long last, our city's public security problems had been solved, and promptly split into separate groups to apply our minds – there were nine of us at this point – to other pressing issues that required our attention. Two of us conducted an investigation; three of us engaged in research; the other four sank into wild cogitation. But just as our three groups began drafting letters based on the fruits of our investigations, research, and cogitation, and as our three groups began to draft our three letters of advice, we found that the state of law enforcement in the city remained grim.

We knew, of course, that the size and scope of the problems facing municipal law enforcement meant that they might never be completely resolved. Naive – not to say childlike – we may have been, but we still lived in the same society as everybody else, and we knew enough to be sceptical of utopias and panaceas. Still, the negligible effect of the new CrackCom order on night-time crime rates came as a shock to us. Statistics showed a nearly vertical drop-off in crimes related to the 'three vehicles' – buses, motorbikes, and bicycles – but a nearly vertical increase in unrelated crimes, as if the miscreants who'd been committing vehicle-related crimes had suddenly all decided to move into new lines of criminality.

First among these was an upswing in brawls: at roadside kebab stands, in street-side parks, at night market stalls, outside the entrances of internet cafes – anywhere crowds of people gathered for fun, shoving would turn to arguments, would turn to shouting, would turn to cursing, would turn to bloodshed. Second was an increase in rape. Not all the women on the streets after 8pm were able to take cabs, or might not find it so easy to get that second two-thirds reimbursed, and a lack of transportation meant more women spending more time in dangerous areas, which meant more targets for sex offenders. Breaking and entering was up: without transportation, many people didn't get home from work until late in the evening, providing a window of opportunity for criminal elements to climb onto balconies, squeeze through windows, pry doors off the hinges, drill locks, and strip homes bare – in some cases arranging for moving trucks to haul away their takings. Following the promulgation of the CrackCom order, overall crime was down from the previous summer by one-fifth across the city, but brawls, rapes, and robberies had increased by one-fifth, three-fifths of a fifth, and five-tenths of a fifth, respectively.

The nine of us reconvened: what to do? Social order was the most pressing issue of the day, and we devoted all of our free time to thought on this new front. This resulted in a new letter, and upon learning that our city's highest-ranking municipal administrator would attend a ribbon-cutting ceremony for a new bathhouse, we took collective, concealed, coordinated action. One of us darted forward, lightning-fast, delivering the letter directly and vanishing back into the crowd before the highest-ranking municipal administrator's three bodyguards and three secretaries could stop him. In addition to our usual report on on-the-ground conditions, this letter put forth several suggestions, including cancelling restrictions on the 'three vehicles,' removing the current ineffectual head of CrackCom and appointing a new CrackCom leader who might be more effective, and expanding the police force to guarantee no fewer than three patrolmen per square kilometre. We had twelve suggestions in all, several of them eminently practicable.

Not all of these were the product of unanimous agreement. The nine of us had originally planned to write separate letters, as usual, with different groups signing their names to letters representing their own viewpoints. The circumstances of this letter, however, seemed clearly to require an exception. Even if we got past the secretaries and bodyguards, we could hardly expect the highest-ranking municipal administrator to stand there next to the young female emcee, holding his oversized pair of golden scissors, celebratory firecrackers going off on all sides, while we each submitted our own letter – and presenting a united front with a joint letter might underscore the importance of the letter and convince the highest-ranking municipal administrator to take it more seriously. And so, in an unprecedented turn of events, we composed a joint letter without unanimous agreement on its content. Our disagreements were on points of principle, naturally, rather than on fundamental issues. Democratically minded intellectuals that we were, we took pains to indicate at the end of the letter which signatories agreed with which suggestions.

This time we saw no immediate effect. Days passed, and CrackCom continued to implement the original regulation. The office's revised recommendations made the regulation more palatable to the general public, but did nothing to address the newly created problems of social order. Brawling, rape, and robbery continued to fill the nights with terror and besmirch the civility and social harmony of our city.

Our minds raced. We had never worried too much about the letters that we'd sent out before, since any misgivings we might have could be explained by the possibility that the highest-ranking municipal administrator had never received the letter. After all, he worked night and day with the pressures of a thousand weighty matters bearing down upon him; where would he find the time to read a letter from a group of nobodies? This time we knew to a moral certainty that he had received the letter himself – so why, when he had always responded to us through real-world policy changes in the past, was there now only silence? Some among us suggested that we write another letter, something more strongly worded than the last, but most of us were against this – indeed, one of us suggested worriedly that we not get ideas above our stations. After careful reflection, we decided unanimously that the highest-ranking municipal administrator had read our letter and chosen not to take any of our suggestions – possibly out of annoyance at us, and quite possibly out of annoyance at the way we had delivered the letter. We guessed, also, that the CrackCom director we had judged ineffectual might keep his position and could retaliate against us at any time – his background was something of an open secret, and his backers outranked those of the highest-ranking municipal administrator. And after all, we weren't as young as we had been. Our passions had cooled, our impulsiveness given way to rationality. Memories of our time as the focus of the municipal PSB's attentions elicited a twinge or two of retrospective terror. In the end, the people who had advocated writing another letter abandoned the idea owing to a lack of support and a shortage of new suggestions.

At the same time, of course, we reproached ourselves for our timidity and selfish hesitation. As patriotic intellectuals concerned for our country and our fellow citizens, we felt, we lacked the craft and courage of our literati forebears, who staked their lives on their words. For a while, our loosely knit collective threatened to fall apart in a storm of recriminations. Our manners may have been the only thing that kept us together – all of us were too embarrassed to make the first move to disband the group, secretly hoping it would happen through a gradual distancing and cooling, a shifting of the subject, a slow disassociation.

It was just at this time that CrackCom issued a new regulation, which the three mouthpieces of state media promptly broadcast at full volume, and at once we were back to our old selves again, like balloons re-inflating. Regardless of the content of the regulation, our letter had produced at least one visible effect: the new CrackCom regulation bore a new signature. We couldn't help but blame ourselves once again, this time for our lack of faith. As for the original director of CrackCom, there was a sense of concern that we might have ended his career with our focus on his shortcomings. Not until we heard that he had taken up a new position – a minor promotion, albeit to a post without many of the perks of his former job – did our sense of guilt lessen slightly. We debated whether or not to write another letter to the highest-ranking municipal administrator expressing our thanks in the form of a poem, but our newfound caution convinced us not to write.

The new regulation was: in addition to strict enforcement of the previous regulation, all individuals engaged in outdoor activity between the hours of 8pm and 5am would be required to do so while squatting.

...To do so while squatting? How were people supposed to do everything squatting? *Why* were people supposed to do everything squatting? Wasn't the ability to rise from a squat to a stand the very quality that separated men from apes? The broad masses of the public didn't understand or accept the new regulation, and expressed their discontent through murmurs and grumbles and other means of silent protest. The nine of us, however, being more incisive thinkers – I'm sorry, but we really are just a bit smarter than most – instantly understood the reasoning behind the new requirement, which was precisely the same as that offered by the mass media.

First, the drawbacks. There are two major drawbacks to

doing things while squatting: how much slower it renders all movement, and the numb legs and aching joints that result from protracted squatting. The negative aspects of squatting are familiar to everyone and will require no further description – unlike the positives, which merit further enumeration. The positive aspects of squatting are complementary to the negative aspects: slow movement, numb legs, and sore joints are objectively positive factors in preventing criminal elements from committing crimes. A group of drunks looking for a fight, for instance, will shortly ascertain that a persistent squatting position renders one unable to move with any physical strength. Even if armed with knives, they will find that the sudden motion of attacking meets with painful protest from their numbed, cramping legs, causing them to drop their knife hands reflexively to maintain balance, and nipping neatly in the bud what might have otherwise been a bloody incident. Imagine a rapist squat-rushing at a woman in short, mincing steps, backing her into a corner, and then —but how would sexual relations occur between two squatting people? Of course, the rapist could throw the woman to the ground and throw himself on top of her, but even ignoring the effects of protracted squatting on the human sex drive and sexual performance, how intimidating could a lowlife be, so close to the ground? Especially when the woman could resist by simply standing up —an option open to her, but not him, under the same legal principle permitting violence in the cause of legitimate self-defence? Even if he dared stand up, patrolmen would descend upon him for violating the regulation before circulation ever returned to his legs, and our would-be rapist would be worse off than when he had started. Imagine a group of thieves planning to rob the empty home of a wealthy man. They have done reconnaissance, planned their escape route, prepared a car to transport their takings and a full set of pliers, screwdrivers, crowbars, scissors, and other implements of crime; they have waited for just the right moment, and now – but how are they to get up onto the balcony? How will they squeeze through the window? Their sole option will be to enter the building and attempt to pry the iron anti-theft door off its frame, a time-consuming and difficult proposition. Any ideas of climbing onto a balcony or squeezing through the window are doomed to failure: either of these would require them to stand up straight while outdoors, a move that would instantly mark them as thieves to any law-abiding citizen or police officer within the vicinity. Clearly, evil-doers of all varieties would find their ambitions thwarted, were squatting to be generally enforced.

It took only a week for the results of the new regulation to become clear in the form of a pronounced improvement in the state of public security in our city. Criminals of all kinds had simply scattered in all directions and vanished without a trace, like cockroaches after the light comes on. It appeared that squatting was a true panacea for crime. Some of the more arrogant criminals, lacking a full appreciation for the seriousness of squatting, continued in their wanton behaviour, but no sooner had they made their move − which is to say, before they had left the scene of the crime and in some cases before the crime had even been committed − than they were caught red-handed by patrolmen. Some would even manage to flee the scene, but the act of standing, even under cover of darkness, caused them to be noticed and promptly reported by law-abiding members of the public, and in the end all were caught up in the sweeping nets of justice. As you can imagine, all eyes will instantly lock onto a man who stands while everyone else is squatting, and he will be left with nowhere to hide.

But after our initial excitement had abated and we had reflected upon our individual experiences, we came to feel that there was a major flaw in the new squatting regulation. For the majority of the public that had no criminal designs, the matter of numb legs and sore joints was a minor one, and easily addressed with a bit of rest, a slap or two with the hands, some rubbing and stretching − but the slowness the squatting caused was an intolerable inconvenience. An example. When a girlfriend came to visit me at my home one night, the security guard at the gate of my residential compound refused to allow her cab to enter the development. Her only option was to disembark and enter the gate at the northwest corner of the compound, squat down, and proceed towards Building 23, where I lived. Building 23 was in the southeast corner of the compound. She had walked there from the northwest corner of the compound before. While large, the compound could be traversed in three to five minutes. But this time, she had to do it in a squat, simultaneously contending with high heels, a long dress, long hair that kept spilling down over her face, and a handbag that kept slipping off her shoulder no matter how she carried it, all of which contributed to her bursting into tears halfway across the compound. It was a full twenty minutes before she arrived inside the gateway of my building and was able to stand up straight again. I asked her why she hadn't called for me to go down and get her, and she replied, still sobbing: 'Wha- what g-good would th- that do when you d-don't have a c-car? You'd j-just be keeping me c-company...'

She referred to squat-walking as 'crawling.' She crawled over to my bed and started crying her heart out, and wouldn't let me wipe her tears away. We only got to spend the night together once every couple of weeks, and all she did that night was cry.

After compiling together many such reports, we wrote another letter to the highest-ranking municipal administrator to express our firm opposition to the squatting regulation. In heated tones, we said that preventing crime by forcing citizens to squat-walk was a modern variation on the fable of the man who swore off food for fear of choking, or of the policy that would kill 3,000 innocent men to prevent a single guilty man from escaping, and that continuing to enforce the regulation would hold back the development of our society and inhibit the growth of our city.

But when I say 'we' here, I am being imprecise: it still refers to our group of nine, but although we were by and large of the same mind, there was such disagreement over how to express our sentiments that only one or two of us were willing to co-sign letters. The majority of us opted to write our own letters, and three of us decided that although they supported our views, they would not write any more letters – that is, that they would leave our loose collective.

We knew they must have heard the news – all of us had, though we didn't say anything about it. A few days earlier, the highest-ranking municipal administrator had invited a famous singer to a banquet in our city. She complimented him on the progress our city had made, and joked that the sight of all the people squat-walking under the starry, moonlit night sky made her feel as if she were watching a colossal work of performance art. She called our highest-ranking municipal administrator one of the great postmodern artists of our time. Recognizing a kindred spirit, the highest-ranking municipal administrator replied unhappily that he had worn himself out in the cause of promoting good and repressing evil, of protecting the land and securing the common people. But still there were people who, being given an inch and taking a mile, being given a bit of face and taking a whole nose, being insufferably given to picking nits and finding fault wherever they could, were in the habit of constantly writing negative letters. 'I envy you your stalkers,' the highest-ranking municipal administrator sighed to his guest. At least *they* understood love and loyalty. If only the people of his city could be more like them.

The news filled us with a sense of foreboding, but still – times were changing and society was progressing, and if the involvement of the PSB years before hadn't made us fall apart, then we could hardly allow a bit of back-alley gossip to scare us into silence now. On the other hand, since there was strength in numbers and we didn't want to be accused of attempting to sow discontent by sending separate letters, we stuffed the four letters that the remaining six of us had written into a single large envelope and sent them out as one communique. As we mailed the letters off, another two members of our group told us this would be their last letter to the highest-ranking municipal administrator.

Our sense of foreboding was basically correct. As I said, we are more incisive thinkers than most. Two weeks went by without any sign that the highest-ranking municipal administrator had considered our views – but on the other hand we didn't see any signs of a new investigation into us, either. There were only four of us left, and two were married to each other. Many evenings we gathered together in a high building that overlooked the streets, and gazed out to see, under the shimmering lights, parallel to the streams of vehicles, on the streets that stretched out as far as the eyes could see, the ever more familiar sight of crowds of men and women, young and old, shifting their weight from side to side and rocking backward and forward as they squat-walked to and fro. It was a funny sight, but we weren't laughing. We knew that if we needed to go out to work or visit friends or family, and we couldn't catch a ride with a friend or put together money for a cab, then we would join the freaks squat-walking outside. Even as we stood inside, looking out from the air-conditioned comfort of the apartment, we might already be among them. It was a chilling, gloomy realization.

We wrote another letter, a joint missive signed by the four of us. We expressed our firm moral convictions by means of heated, even confrontational language – phrases like 'human dignity,' 'the difference between man and beast,' 'no different from mindless tortoises,' 'slowness equals death,' and 'adapting to numbness is a sign of a tacit acceptance of atrophy and regression.' We even wrote that 'an even surer way to protect the streets might be to keep the entire populace as house pets, or to declare martial law outright.' But after finishing, we looked at each other and decided we didn't have the courage to mail off anything so fiery. After a long silence, the wife in the husband and wife couple – our group's only female member, the bright young computing prodigy who had joined us all those years before – burst into tears.

'Why don't we just play mahjong?' she said. 'We've got the right number of people.'

And so we began to enliven our otherwise dull night lives with our newfound hobby of mahjong – no wonder so many people found it addictive. One evening, as we searched under the sofa for a dropped tile, we found the letter that we had written but never sent out. After reading the letter again, we all agreed that despite a certain elegance and moral force, it was undeniably a work of juvenilia – trite, ill-considered, focusing on details at the expense of the big picture.

As we played round after happy round of mahjong one evening, two of our old comrades – the two who had sent out the last letter with us – called to say they'd heard we were all together, and to ask if they could drop by. We'd missed them since their departure, we said, but it was already 10 pm, and to get to where we were gathered there was a stretch of road that cabs were barred from, meaning they'd have to cover the distance in a squat. Our mahjong club usually got together before 8pm so that we could avoid squat-walking. Never mind that, they said. Just wait for us.

We assumed they wouldn't arrive before 11, but at 10:17 there they were – driving, each in his own car! They grinned wildly as they parked their cars beside our building so that they only had to squat-walk for ten or twenty metres before stepping inside and stretching their limbs to stand back up in front of us. They had become members of the driving classes, and night-time excursions no longer presented any inconvenience to them.

We were by no means poor, intellectuals that we were, but neither were we politicians or big shots. Though tempted to join the growing number of private car owners, we had decided to wait and learn to drive first, and to date this was as far as any of us had allowed ourselves to go. Partly this was out of a desire to wait until prices fell; partly it was because new expenses kept cropping up – new houses to replace old work-unit housing, private school tuition for children, savings to help parents enjoy a comfortable retirement – and none of us felt particularly wealthy. So how had these two become big spenders?

They sat down across from us and explained how they had come to buy the cars. Big spending didn't enter into it, they said: their new luxury cars had been practically free, thanks to special vouchers they'd been given by the director of CrackCom. This flummoxed us – what did cars have to do with CrackCom, and why would they have vouchers from CrackCom anyway?

They squirmed a little at the question.

'Maybe the letter?' one of them said.

The last letter we wrote to the highest-ranking municipal administrator? we said. But we wrote to him too, we said. How come *we* didn't get anything?

Their new car-owning self-assurance returned, and they began to look amused.

'—You want to join the driving classes too, is that it?'

But before we could accuse them of having forgotten who their friends were, they leaned forward earnestly.

'After all the years we've known each other, after all we've done together,' said the one who was the lover of the highest-ranking municipal administrator's secretary's wife, 'what's ours is yours. We were just worried that you were going to say we'd sold out, or that we'd just driven over here to lord it over you. You know the saying about the bravest person in human history being the first man to eat a crab? That's us – we tried the bourgeois crab first so you wouldn't have to.'

As he spoke, he pulled out four vouchers authorizing low-cost car purchases and slapped them down on the mahjong table, where we could see the red seal of CrackCom and the signature of the CrackCom director on each.

The secretary's wife's lover explained that a few days earlier he had received a call from the secretary asking him to come in for a chat. Naturally he found this unsettling, but the secretary's wife assured him that he had nothing to worry about – her husband knew they were old classmates, but had no clue that they were sleeping together. So he went and sat down with the husband of his lover, the secretary of the highest-ranking municipal administrator, in an office just across from the administrator's own. After a prodigious amount of small talk and conversation filler, the secretary finally brought up the topic of the squatting regulation.

'I understand that you intellectuals may have a hard time getting used to the regulation,' he said. 'The leaders don't have to squat, because they have cars; the big shots don't have to squat, because *they* have cars; the labouring classes mostly don't mind squatting because they've got strong knees and waists, but you intellectuals... CrackCom has made an internal decision to periodically offer batches of high-quality cars to select intellectuals at borderline suicidal discounts – so what do you say? If you're interested, I'll get the director of CrackCom to write you out a voucher right now.'

'Not interested,' our comrade nobly replied without giving the offer even a moment's thought. 'There are plenty of intellectuals out there like me, and if they have to squat, then I'll squat along with them.'

'You're a stand-up guy,' the secretary/husband laughed. 'No wonder my wife is always saying good things about you. How about this: there are five cars in the first batch. I'll get CrackCom to give them all to you, and if five's not enough then you can have the second and third batches too. How about that? Any problems with that arrangement?'

Our comrade immediately called the other comrade who had left our group with him, and they went to CrackCom to get their vouchers. Instead of startling us with the sudden news, the two decided that they would each take a car home first. After 8pm they took their new cars out for a long spin around the city. Then they called us.

The four of us rushed forward to shake their hands. Tears filled our eyes as emotion overwhelmed us.

Our sole female member broke the silence some moments later, her eyes sparkling as she stroked one of the vouchers with a fingertip.

'Even if he' – she meant the secretary/husband – 'didn't mention the letter, it's obviously what all this is about. But' – she laid a hand gently on her husband's chest – 'how on Earth could he have known that two of the six authors were married to each other? And that no matter how cheap the cars were, the married couple would only be able to afford one?'

She spoke seriously, but we all laughed, including her husband. Sometimes being a little naive, a little silly, a little dumb, just makes women more loveable. Even if they're former computer geniuses.

In no time at all, we became members of the car-owning classes. The five of us would go out for drives together, enjoying our new status. When we got together in the evenings, we could drive wherever and whenever we wanted, without having to concern ourselves with being unable to take a cab down this street, or having to squat-walk down that street. So far as squat-walking was concerned, I had it better than the others: there were times when they couldn't avoid squat-walking – like when the two of us who had first received cars had come to visit: they'd still had to hunker down and squat-walk the ten or twenty metres from their cars to the doorway. It was a short distance, and it was inside the residential compound, but not squatting was still against the rules. I, on the other hand, had simply hired a chauffeur, since I'd never learned to drive. When I came or went, the chauffeur would drive to the front of my building. The burden of squat-walking to and from the parked car was his, and I never had to squat down again – one long stride would be sufficient to carry me from my building into the car, or from the car back into the building.

My comrades joked that I was acting like a leader or a big shot. They were right – leaders and big shots had chauffeurs and people to do the squatting for them, too.

'Never mind leaders and big shots,' our sole female member said. 'Why not just say he's acting like me?'

We laughed, after a moment of surprised silence. That was our former computer genius – an analytical thinker. She was right, I was like her. Her husband was her chauffeur, and any place or any time she didn't feel like it, she didn't have to squat down either.

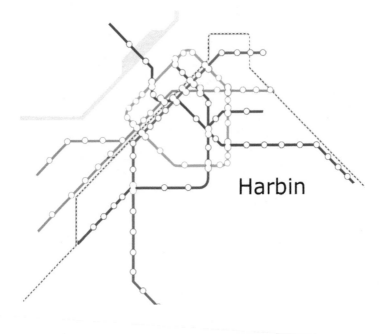

Harbin

How To Look At Women

ZHU WEN

TRANSLATED BY JULIA LOVELL

ALLOW ME TO introduce my friend Xiao Liu. His real name is Liu Guixiang and he'll be fifty this year.[7] He was born in the year of the ox, which makes him a whole lunar cycle and a half older than me, and works in the I.T. department of the Soil Research Institute here in Nanjing. He received some semblance of a further education at the end of the Cultural Revolution, spending two years at the Nanjing Workers' College (now Southeast University) in the department of mechanical engineering, after which he was assigned by our wonderful state planners to the Soil Research Institute (to a job which had, naturally, not a blessed thing to do with anything he had previously studied). His lack of a proper degree had vexed him ever since Mao and his mischief-making educational policies came to an end, until finally in 1988 he managed to get a BA by correspondence course. That year, he also turned thirty-nine and joined the Party. He told me at the time (and I recall several other forty-something friends saying something similar, so let it count as a representative symptom of midlife crisis) that he'd been doing some long-term thinking recently: he still had hopes of getting a job in local government and a slightly bigger apartment.

Unfortunately, a string of distracting misfortunes came his way. First his six-year-old son Liu Gang got tubercular

7. 'Xiao' adds an affectionate diminutive to his surname, Liu.

169

meningitis, then his elderly father died, then his younger sister got her leg crushed in a motorcycle accident and had to come to Nanjing for an operation. Finally, at the end of that *annus horribilis*, he separated from his wife Lin Zhimin, a local Nanjinger and an accountant in the Irrigation Research Bureau. Three years later, they divorced, with the court giving him custody of their son. Xiao Liu explained the causes of the rupture in only the sketchiest terms. The two of them had never rubbed along particularly well, he told me; they were always arguing about one thing or another. At the end of each of their regular rows, she'd fling some clothes into a bag and retreat to her parents' place for a fortnight. I'm sure that Xiao Liu sometimes deliberately provoked arguments just to get a rest. So the news of their break-up wasn't a shock; what surprised me was that Xiao Liu had the resolve to get a divorce. Of course, it was Lin Zhimin who pushed it through: as soon as things loosened up after the death of Mao, she found herself a lover, though Xiao Liu didn't discover this (and in his own marital bed too) till deep into the 1980s.

It was a little before this that he'd discovered why the water kept cutting out on the top floors of his apartment building. He'd just been transferred to the Housing Department in the Soil Research Institute, and his head of department had put him in charge of improving the older buildings in the residential compounds. He'd been obsessed with radios since high school; he lived and breathed multimeters, soldering irons and diodes, and had a decent, hands-on understanding of how they worked. After a little jiggery-pokery and the addition of a pressure pump, he came up with a device that meant inhabitants of the fourth floor and above never needed to worry about the water supply again. This represented, I understood, the pinnacle of Xiao Liu's engineering career, although he later had a minor stroke of genius over television circuits, apparently improving their efficiency by seventy percent. Once confirmed by a succession of relevant experts, his innovation was included in that year's Provincial Plan for

Strategic Technology. Although he later seemed rather embarrassed by this success, at the time his invention improved his life in a number of ways. The senior management initially remained oblivious to its potential, probably because neither they nor any of their relatives lived above the third floor. But news of the contraption spread like wildfire, and several households from upper storeys asked Xiao Liu to come and fix their water supply problems. Xiao Liu charged a hundred yuan – including labour and materials – for each pressure-pump that he fitted, meaning that he made more than fifty yuan on each device. Each staircase with this problem needed one of his pressure pumps; and each department in the Institute had several dodgy old buildings.

Soon Xiao Liu needed an assistant – which is where I came into the picture. We'd work nights together, assembling the parts; I wasn't capable of much more than the finishings, but it was all fiddly, manual work. So I suggested that he raised the price, to 150 yuan a throw. Xiao Liu struck his forehead: 'Of course – why didn't I think of that?' They still sold like hot cakes, even at the new price; so we raised it to 200. At this, he became a little uneasy; 'What next?' he asked me, '250?' When Xiao Liu's Head of Department got wind of Xiao Liu's second stream of income, he was furious until he got a better idea. He detailed two employees to Xiao Liu to help him with installation and negotiated a cut for the department. Even though the department was now creaming off most of the profits, Xiao Liu felt he was doing well enough out of it – maybe he was making a bit less than before, but he felt more comfortable about it. And he got to use the departmental tools and workshop space.

The Head of Housing was considerably savvier than Xiao Liu – he quickly realised this was worth getting a patent for. (Up to this point, Xiao Liu had simply been smearing the circuit boards and internal parts of all installed pumps with black ink to keep his trade secret from others). But as soon as Xiao Liu went to consult the new provincial patents bureau, he got cold feet: he discovered that applying cost money – around 2,000 yuan. At this moment, his head of department generously decided to advance the money himself and the patent was quickly approved, granted jointly to Xiao Liu and the Soil Research Institute Housing Department. (Xiao Liu was not particularly delighted about this: what had the Housing Department ever invented?) Seized by the entrepreneurial spirit then sweeping the country, the Head of Housing applied for an Institute loan to start a factory, to produce the pumps on an industrial scale; and Xiao Liu stopped grumbling after he got promoted to the rank of mid-level technician. The senior management at the Soil Research Institute – which was one big financial black hole – were naturally delighted at the prospect of a moneymaking opportunity. But as soon as preparations were underway, they encountered a problem which on the surface was a disagreement about naming the product, but in reality went far deeper – Xiao Liu's head of department had been avoiding the subject of how much of the profit from this new venture was to go to the inventor. Anyway, Xiao Liu wanted the pump named after him. The head of department countered that such an idea was vulgar individualism. The director of the Institute finally intervened by choosing the 'Good Earth', which contained a highly pertinent reference to soil while sounding auspiciously expansive. Although Xiao Liu wasn't happy about it, there wasn't much he could do about it.

Just when the loan had been approved, a new product burst onto the market, The King of Faucets, which shared many similarities with the Good Earth while managing to be considerably cheaper. What Facebook was to the Winklevoss twins, the King of Faucets was to Xiao Liu. The head of department bought one and asked Xiao Liu to check it out; he was sure their design had been ripped off and was totally ready to sue. Three months of frenetic litigation later, the Good Earth Pressure Pump factory closed before it had even opened. The King of Faucets management produced a wad of documentation proving that their product had been patented before the Good Earth. They warned the Soil Institute that if they went ahead manufacturing their Good Earth Pressure Pump, they'd sue *their* asses for infringement of copyright. While all this was going on, the King of Faucets even managed to bring out an improved, second generation model. When the National Patents' office told Xiao Liu they were thinking of cancelling his certificate, Xiao Liu dropped the whole thing; if he lost the patent, would he lose his promotion too? Was the King of Faucets going to sue him for all the pumps he'd already installed? His love affair with radio technology crumbled to dust and nothingness. In all the years he'd been messing about with radios, all he'd managed to invent was something someone else had already thought of. He promptly switched his allegiance to computers.

So the Head of Housing's get-rich-quick scheme was aborted. He tore his copy of the patent certificate in two, threw it in the bin, and settled down to wait quietly for retirement. He had several powerful analogies for the new socio-economic phenomenon of patents, Xiao Liu – who took this setback much better than his boss – told me. 'You see a woman walking along the street,' he'd counselled Xiao Liu when he was originally getting him to apply. 'Even if no one else has seen her, she isn't yours yet. So you smear ink all over her face – but other men can still smell her. Hide her in a hole underground, and she's still no use to you because she's not yours yet. Stand guard over her with a gun and you're still not safe – the moment you go off for a piss, she'll have run off with someone else. That's why you have to get a marriage licence. That way, she's yours. A patent's just like that: it means other men can only look, not touch. And you have to act fast, because there are lots of other men out there with eyes in their heads. Twig?' After the litigation debacle, the Head of Housing's logic took on a more melancholic tone: 'You see a woman walking down the street; anyone can look at her, but only the first person to see her can have her. A patent's just like that.

Twig?' Xiao Liu would later come to feel that his Head of Department's sage similes had laid the imaginative groundwork for his own divorce, which he took much more easily as a result.

I was only seventeen when Xiao Liu dragged me into his business venture. I'd just started college in Nanjing – at Southeast University, his own alma mater, but in a different department (Power Engineering). It was because of Xiao Liu that I'd ended up at a Nanjing college, rather than in Beijing, which I'd set my sights on going to. I'll have more to say about that later. Every time I helped with his business venture, however little I did, Xiao Liu insisted on giving me twenty yuan. To begin with, he'd wanted to pay me thirty, but I managed to haggle him down. And so it was that, after doing almost nothing at all, I had four hundred yuan to my name. My parents wired me forty yuan a month for living expenses; so I'd basically got my hands on a whole year's allowance without even thinking about it. As soon as the New Year holiday arrived, I bought a ticket to Harbin, the frozen city beyond the Great Wall. For one, I had a classmate from Harbin, called Zhang Dong, and we rubbed along pretty well. Secondly, I'd always liked the name Harbin – it sounded exotically remote. When I looked it up in the dictionary, I discovered it was a transliteration into Chinese characters of Russian words meaning Where Fishing Nets Dry.

It did not occur to me even once that a place where you dried fishing nets could also be cold. After the train had passed Shanhaiguan, the easternmost fort in the Great Wall, the desolation of the scenery outside the window forced me to make a realistic projection about Harbin's probable temperature (the train itself was seriously over-centrally heated; it gave me a bad headache, but at least it wasn't cold). As the train moved through the landscape, my forecasts steadily fell. Even so, the coldness exceeded my most extravagant expectations. My first thought on leaving the station was to wonder why on Earth I wasn't wearing more clothes.

Zhang Dong's family lived in a suburban slum of single storey houses: the nine of them were crammed into less than twenty square metres. They had no central heating, of course: the only warmth inside the house came from pipes that ran from the stove into hollow partition walls. My arrival only increased the intense pressure on space and resources in their household. And yet they were irrepressibly hospitable; and the more welcoming they were, the worse I felt. The interior of the house was divided into several small rooms, with the largest given over to Zhang Dong's parents. His father was a retired worker, probably somewhere in his sixties – a patriarch with a savage temper. Every evening, he'd settle down with a flask of warm wine, roaring at his family between sips. It was Zhang Dong's mother who generally got the worst of it. Everywhere they went, Zhang Dong's two married older brothers brought with them beaten tin lunchboxes filled with tobacco. They were as brutal to their wives as their father was to their mother; they spoke only to shout at them. Perhaps Zhang Dong's second brother shouted a little less, partly because he liked to hit his wife too. She spent most of her time by the stove making dumplings, the tears rolling down her bruised face. It was a perfect revelation to me: I had no idea that men could be such emperors in their own homes.

Zhang Dong, my classmate, was a late third son, and the first of the family to get into university. Though he never had a lot to say for himself, he was made much of, so the largest bed in the house was cleared for him and me to sleep on. My first few days there, Zhang Dong took me around the city after breakfast. Because the clothes I'd brought were all too thin for the Harbin winter, I had to borrow a blue wadded-cotton greatcoat belonging to Zhang Dong's father and a shabby fur hat belonging to Zhang Dong's oldest brother. The coat was ripped at the armpit seam, and every few steps I had to pause to stuff the sallow wadding back inside. We'd wander about the city till it got dark, have dinner then go out again to Zhaolin Park where the annual ice and snow festival was on – the park was filled with frozen monuments (mainly animals, or buildings) carved by sculptors from all over the world. By the time we got back, Zhang Dong's family were asleep. Though I got the feeling that Zhang Dong didn't want to spend more time at home than he had to, he didn't seem to want to tell me about it either. Within a couple of days, we'd walked just about everywhere there was to walk: along the Slavonic apartment blocks lining Central Avenue, around Stalin Park and the snow sculptures of Sun Island. I'd also discovered that Harbin's north wind was more than capable of freezing your eyeballs into immobility. I began to wonder if Zhang Dong had packed my schedule this tightly so that I could get my sightseeing done and go home as soon as possible. Maybe he'd only extended his invitation to me casually; maybe he'd never thought I'd be tactless enough to take him up on it. There was no way I could stay till the New Year – it was a long ten days away. But when I suggested I go home, Zhang Dong and his family fiercely fought the idea. How could I think of coming all this way and not staying for New Year? The worry-lines across his mother's forehead visibly deepened: did I think they were too poor to give me anything decent to eat? Was the bed too uncomfortable? I immediately retracted the idea, mortified at their suspicions. I was warmed by the generosity and directness of people from the north of my country, and irritated by my own convoluted, second-guessing southern instincts.

We couldn't go out the next few days after that. The ground-level temperature was so low that the pavements had completely frozen over. And Zhang Dong's family wanted to keep him at home a little more, to enjoy the short, precious holiday time. I tried as hard as I could to reinvent myself as a member of Zhang Dong's family: to enjoy the daily, banal pleasures of life in their home; to appreciate the great good fortune of being able to sit inside, watching the New Year's snow swirl outside the windows. At mealtimes, I gulped down vast quantities of pickled cabbage – a substance I usually shunned – to demonstrate my dedication to the vegetable that dominated their diet; after a few days, I discovered to my surprise, I had taken to it. I could not get the hang of their toilets though. As there was no bathroom in the house, they and their neighbours had to use a semi-exposed communal pit latrine. The inside of the toilet alone – scattered with rods of excrement and icicles of urine – gave me pause. The winter had frozen everything solid – even the smell had been neutralised by the sub-zero temperatures. The pit itself – on which you needed to squat – was carpeted by glistening ice; I was terrified that I would slip on it. You had only a moment to complete your business, before severe frostbite kicked in. When I failed to seize this moment several days in a row, Zhang Dong took me to a toilet in a children's hospital nearby (one stop away) that was – luxury – centrally heated. A tram-stop stood by the main entrance, and every morning as I emerged from the hospital at rush hour, a crowd of people waited beneath the sign, snorting white vapour, stamping their feet. I enjoyed standing there, watching. The faces of Harbin women had larger pores than those of their southern counterparts, and they wore far more foundation; their skin always had a greenish-white tinge to it – I liked it, it made them seem more solid, more real, somehow. The men, by contrast, seemed dull, depressed, enveloped in the smell of tobacco. As I contemplated them, I realised that this breed of woman was forever condemned to this breed of man: they cooked for them, they had their children, they were beaten by them. What must they think of it all?

One figure in particular drew my attention. She was tall – around a metre seventy – and straight-backed; she wore a hip-length red down jacket; her long, slender legs ended in a pair of black riding boots. A black plait hung down her back and her neck was muffled in a white scarf. When the tram arrived, everyone rushed at the doors – except for her. She waited patiently at the back of the crowd. After the tram had left, she stood at the front of those left behind; she glanced in

the direction from which the tram had come, then looked
back out over the street. Because she turned away so fast, I
didn't get a look at her face, though for some reason I got the
idea her eyelashes were very long. By this point, Zhang Dong
was starting to complain at the cold and wanted to hurry on
home; I asked him to let me stay a little longer. But she didn't
turn back around. I began to think perhaps it would be best
if I didn't see her face; she was so alluring from behind, it
would be crushingly disappointing if her face turned out to
be ordinary, or even unattractive. For that, surely, is the way
things always do turn out. The moment I had formulated my
theory, she turned around, as if to refute it: her eyes were a
clear, brilliant blue, slightly sunken, and colder than the
January wind that was gusting around us. My throat tightened;
the blood surged through me. Though she was looking in my
direction, there was something empty in those piercing eyes;
I could find no reflection of myself. Before I had got a proper
look at her face, I had to look away, down at my feet, my face
blazing scarlet, as if she had seen into my soul. I had only a
vague, imperfect sense of her features. I yearned to stand
alongside her – a couple of steps was all it would have taken
– and survey her at my leisure. An instant later, though, I
remembered what I was wearing: the matted hat, the ancient
coat. My courage deserted me: I felt I could not bear to be
noticed by that aquamarine stare, not in my current state. But
at the same time I craved another look at her. I stood there,
paralysed by indecision, allowing my resolve to ebb quietly
away. When the tram finally carried her off, ringing its bell, I
sighed, almost in relief. I remembered Zhang Dong. He had
already set off for home, but had paused a little way ahead to
wait for me, his neck shrunk into his shoulders, his mittened
hands shielding his nose. He motioned with his head, to
indicate that I should catch up.

Zhang Dong didn't seem too fazed by my performance
at the tram-stop; as we walked along, he explained briefly that
she was an 'ermao'. When I failed to understand the local

argot, he enlarged a little. Before the Russian Revolution, a great many refugees had fled to Harbin and settled there. Several generations later, they were completely naturalised; the only thing that distinguished them from the locals was their physiology. Purebred Russians were called 'lao maozi' – literally 'old hairy ones'. But Eurasians, those with mixed Russian and Chinese blood, were called 'ermao', 'second hairy ones'. I asked him if all half-Russians were as beautiful as she was. Some are pig-ugly, Zhang Dong replied. Despite the contempt in his voice, I immediately thought of my favourite Russian literary heroines: Anna Karenina, Tonia from *How The Steel Was Tempered* or Chekhov's heroine in 'Anna On the Neck'. My heart began to beat faster as I nursed the memory of those blue eyes. But I dropped the subject; I didn't want Zhang Dong to think me naïve.

The next day when I went to the toilet, I didn't wear the coat or the fur hat. Zhang Dong's mother told me I couldn't go out like that, that I'd freeze to death. I didn't mind, I replied, it wasn't far and I was going to run – I needed the exercise. Zhang Dong's face twisted with displeasure; I suspected that he'd realised I didn't want to wear his family's old clothes out. But my mind was on other things. He sourly told me I shouldn't be running in this weather, that the air would destroy my lungs; and left it at that. It wasn't as bad as he'd said it would be: although my nose ran with the cold, I felt much better for the brisk run. If I saw my half-Russian again, I was determined to get a proper look at her. Because I now knew the way, Zhang Dong no longer offered to go with me; he visited his toilet, and I visited mine. We were our own people. I enjoyed my freedom, I enjoyed not needing to feel guilty or constrained by his presence. I cherished my only moment of privacy in the day; I even stayed out a little longer than I had to.

For the past few days, Zhang Dong's family had been plotting something together; I sensed, from their expressions, that it was something important. He didn't seem to want to tell me; whenever I was around, Zhang Dong scowled at his family to shut up. 'Why don't you tell your classmate?' his oldest brother's wife blurted out once. Zhang Dong shot her a vicious glare and told her to shut up. I made a point of going through to the next-door room and playing with his nephews.

The closer New Year came, the more conscious I was of how superfluous my presence was. One evening, Zhang Dong's second brother brought home an enormous haunch of pork; the whole family gathered round to admire it. Their New Year's purchases, including the dumplings they'd prepared, were all wrapped in plastic and stored in a lean-to outside the front door, which served as a natural freezer. But every evening at bedtime, they brought the pork haunch inside, to keep it safe from burglars. The rest of the year they never ate so much meat; at most meals it was pickled cabbage and rice noodles sprinkled, at best, with a little chopped bacon. You had to eat their food hot; it became demoralisingly slimy as it cooled. Fresh meat, and other vegetables such as green pepper, were a New Year's treat. Perhaps because it was so cold, I craved meat, great hunks of fatty meat, even though I knew that the family had to scrimp and save for every scrap they consumed. They didn't throw their money about, not because they were mean, but because they just didn't have much. Every time I wanted meat, I felt ashamed of the impulse.

Four days before the New Year, Zhang Dong told me a little mysteriously that he couldn't go out with me that day because there was something he had to go and do with his father. That was fine, I naturally said. He was dressed unusually smartly, I noticed; his father had also swapped his slovenly house-attire for a navy blue wool coat ironed into even, faded creases; the buttons were gleaming with gilt, except for the plastic one on the lefthand sleeve that must have replaced one that had fallen off. He'd even shaved, and carefully; the few surviving salt and pepper bristles on his chin were pointed out by his grandson. After feeling for them, he tried to pluck them then went out, coughing as usual. Zhang Dong followed behind, carefully carrying two bottles of wine and a beribboned, boxed gift. I felt particularly oppressed that day, alone in this house that wasn't mine, waiting to be fed; but neither could I complain at being neglected. At midday, Zhang Dong's older sister-in-law told me in a whisper that Zhang Dong had gone to meet his fiancée. 'It's all been agreed for ages now, but we've been waiting for him to come home so the two of them can meet.'

'Whose fiancée?' I asked stupidly.

'Zhang Dong's, I told you; his father's getting on and he wants to get it all sorted so he doesn't have to worry. Don't be angry that he's gone out without you.'

'Of course not,' I quickly said.

She looked keenly at me: 'Please don't let on to Zhang Dong that I told you, or he'll shout at me. I think he's worried about his classmates laughing at him.'

'Does Zhang Dong shout too?' I asked her, surprised.

'After his father, he's got the worst temper of all of them,' she replied.

The two of them didn't return until dusk was about to become night. His father, who had clearly had a lot to drink, was shouting even more than usual, yelling at his wife to get the bed ready because he wanted to go to sleep.

'What about dinner?' she asked.

'My fair lady,' he suddenly sang out in operatic style, 'I am replete.'

Zhang Dong also seemed to have been drinking; he was flushed red down to the base of his neck. He sat on the edge of the bed, staring straight out in front of him. The family gathered in the central room to discuss the day. A general air of satisfaction prevailed; everyone seemed perfectly content with how the introduction had gone. (And indeed, Zhang Dong married her as soon as he graduated; the following year, they had a daughter. Zhang Dong's father was delighted: he had wanted a granddaughter as well as the two grandsons he already had, and Zhang Dong had duly obliged. The year after that, he died happily of myocardial infarction). To enable them to speak freely, I put on the family's great-coat and headed out. Though I'd originally intended to visit the toilet, I found myself wandering further and further away.

Asking for directions at every block I passed, and after several changes of bus, I finally found my way to the train station. All the tickets going south for New Year were already sold out; but by paying an extra fifty yuan, I got hold of a ticket to Shanghai for the 28th from a ticket tout. Although there was no seat with it, I felt much happier once I had the piece of paper in my hand. By the time I got back to Zhang Dong's, it was nine o'clock (I lost my way in the darkness and snow; it was only the Children's Hospital that gave me back my bearings). Zhang Dong's mother, sisters-in-law and nephews were sitting beneath the lamps; the table was still laid for dinner. The moment I stepped in the door, they all relaxed. Where had I gone, Zhang Dong's mother scolded me, and why hadn't I told them? All the men had gone out looking for me, even Zhang Dong's father. Appalled by the trouble I'd caused, I decided not to tell the truth – I said I'd just gone out for a stroll. The older sister-in-law told me that I needed to be more careful: Harbin wasn't safe, there were a lot of muggings, especially of people who weren't locals. I could have been stabbed to death, buried beneath the snow, and no one would have been the wiser till Spring. While they were telling me this, Zhang Dong's father came back, took off his hat and brushed the snow off. After staring silently at me, he went into his room. His daughters-in-law quickly stood and moved their stools to let him by. I also got up as fast as I could, pressing myself against the wall. After another while, Zhang Dong and his brothers came back separately, their noses blueish-white and red with cold. The younger sister-in-law went to the stove to warm the dinner, because no one had eaten yet. Zhang Dong's mother told the two children to go straight to bed. They didn't want to go: my absence had meant they could stay up later than usual. While we ate, Zhang Dong's father coughed rhythmically next door. Zhang Dong's mother remarked, a little peevishly, that he must have caught cold. I felt horribly guilty. I wanted them to yell at me, to ease my conscience. But no one would. Zhang Dong and his poker-faced brothers refused to say anything at all. They ate noisily, drank their soup and blew their noses.

When we finally went to bed, Zhang Dong asked me, in hushed tones in the dark, if I'd gone to the station.

'How did you know?' I asked him, in surprise.

'Did you get a ticket?' he next asked, without answering my question.

'Yes,' I told him, 'for the day after tomorrow, in the afternoon.'

Zhang Dong tossed and turned a while, without saying anything else. I knew he was unhappy. We were sleeping under a single quilt, and so I felt every ripple of his discontent. But for days now I'd not been sure whether his family wanted me to stay or not; I wasn't really to blame. While I was being scalded in and out of consciousness by the heated wall I lay against, Zhang Dong rolled himself up into a sitting position and told me that I should have told him if I was going to the train station; that he would have gone with me.

'Why did you go on your own?' he suddenly shouted. Everyone in the house would have heard him. I also quickly sat up. After some groping beneath the quilt, I finally found his arm and tugged at it placatingly. I hadn't planned to go to the station, I told him, it had just happened. He remained disconcertingly silent, awaiting the next stage of my explanation. It's true what they say: that one lie leads to another and I now had to explain a whole spectrum of falsified coincidences to Zhang Dong.

Foggy with sleep, I decided to follow the narrative drift of the half-waking dream I had just been having.

'Do you remember the ermao we saw the other day? I'd gone to the Children's Hospital and was about to head home, when I saw her rushing past me to the tram-stop, where the number 41 was pulling in. She seemed to be enveloped in perfume; I reeled from the smell. She stood by the back door of the tram, then ran up to the front and got on. If I didn't get a proper look at her this time, I thought, I'd never get another chance. I squeezed on, just as the doors were about to shut. I tried to edge my way to the front, but it was very crowded, and everyone was swollen with clothing. Though I craned my neck forwards, she was hemmed in on all sides. All I could see was a row of hands clinging onto the supports from the ceiling. But I was sure I recognised her hand, its translucent skin threaded with pale blue veins. I had the strange idea that it wasn't blood inside them: that it was some kind of half-Russian moonshine. Some people got off at the next stop and I grabbed the opportunity to move up the vehicle. I felt I was getting closer and closer, that soon I could feast my eyes on her. When finally we were shoulder to shoulder, I wondered whether I should pluck up the courage to speak to her. As I shunned the idea, she got off; I went on following her, keeping a careful distance all the while so that she wouldn't notice. When she walked, I walked too; when she took buses, I took the same ones. When it got dark, I narrowed the distance between us, to avoid losing her; when the streetlights came on, I retreated a few steps. I never took my eyes off her; it was as if she had branded herself on my pupils. The wind – sharpened with grit and snowflakes – sanded my eyes; but every tear that oozed out carried a reflection of her image. I had no idea where I was and no interest in the points of the compass; all that mattered was that she was in front of me. I didn't realise I'd arrived at the square in front of the station until someone approached and tried to peddle a train ticket.' I had exhausted Zhang Dong's patience.

'What's so special about a half-caste,' he interrupted, lying back down. He tossed and turned a few more times, managing to steal most of the quilt. I didn't know whether he believed me or not; I'd managed to convince myself.

Two days later, still objecting strenuously to my early departure, Zhang Dong's family presented me with three heads of pickled cabbage as a parting gift. ('You won't get them in the South,' Zhang Dong's mother told me). I got on my train, full of guilty regret and conscious that I faced forty hours of intense, jolting discomfort before I'd be back in Nanjing. After we'd gone back through the Great Wall at Shanhaiguan, the cabbage began to defrost; a trail of vegetable juice snaked persistently across the corridor from where I was standing. The train stewardess was a young woman from Harbin, her voice and features similar to those of Zhang Dong's oldest sister-in-law, which misled me into feeling warmer towards her than she did towards me. In fact, she'd taken badly against me on account of the decomposing pickles, and told me to hang the plastic bag containing the cabbages outside the train window. I was dizzy and nauseous from the train's central heating; I started to feel nostalgic for the far more restrained warmth of Zhang Dong's house. My memories of my Harbin trip coalesced into a single, translucent ice sculpture, in the form of my half-Russian. The more I thought about it, the more adamant I became that I had seen her statue at the ice festival in Zhaolin Park. Once I'd reimagined her immortalised in ice, my mental image of her became even harder, even whiter – as if she were cut from marble.

Another trickle of water ambled across the aisle. The stewardess now properly lost her temper at me as she aggressively mopped the area. Smarting at the injustice, I looked under my seat but found nothing that could explain the leak. I'd stood for five long hours to get this seat and my calves were still numb from it. Lacking the strength to engage with the stewardess, I closed my eyes and leaned back against the headrest. Five minutes later, she kicked my cramped calves.

'Look!' she shouted.

I focussed my bleary eyes uncomprehendingly on her. I'd seen quite enough of her self-righteous face; I'd already noted that a tiny black mole shone through the thick blanket of foundation on her right cheek – what else did she want from me? She jabbed the mop violently between my legs; when I looked down, I was astounded to find yet another pool of water there. I quickly stood up and began desperately trying to explain to her that it was nothing to do with me – there was nothing under my seat that could have generated the leak.

'Well, where is it coming from then?' she asked.

'I don't know,' I replied. 'I've been asleep.' The stewardess turned her inquiring gaze on the passengers around me, but as there seemed to be no clear connection between them and the incident in question, they could enjoy their status as innocent bystanders. The stewardess replaced the sodden mop in a lead bucket then glared suspiciously at me again: 'Why is it by *your* foot?' Every passenger in the carriage seemed to be staring at me. My ears burned; I asked her what she was trying to say. The stewardess's forehead knotted with disgust: 'You know exactly what.' She picked up the bucket and stormed off.

I watched in horror as she disappeared up the other end of the carriage, contemplating whether to smash the train window open with my head and jump out. A small trolley laden with stewed chicken legs and liquor bottles nudged insistently at my heel; a male steward stood behind it, clutching a handful of grotty ten-cent notes, silently waiting, head tilted to one side, for me to move. I sat down and took some deep breaths. I lifted my right foot, and then my left, and examined the soles of my shoes; I glanced surreptitiously at my crotch; nothing unusual to report. An old man sitting diagonally opposite me smoking an old-fashioned pipe was shaking his head at me when I looked up again, warning me not to pick a fight with the stewardess. I almost choked with gratitude at this demonstration of sympathy. He liked to squat on his seat with his shoes still on, like a turtle dove, and had been scolded several times for it by the same stewardess, hence his display of solidarity. Feeling marginally better, I leaned back against the headrest once more and closed my eyes. But still I felt anxious; every now and then I'd check under my feet. Even if I managed to sleep, I remembered, I still wouldn't be back in Nanjing when I woke up. Someone was shouting at me. I opened my eyes and discovered it was the old man, squatting on his seat again, his trouser legs rolled up to his knees, revealing the skin – desiccated into fish scales – on his shins. Using his pipe – from which a pouch of tobacco was hanging – he gestured at the area beneath my feet. Another puddle of water had formed and was just beginning to spread.

I had no idea where the water was coming from. I studied the faces of the passengers around me. They all seemed to be delighting in my misfortunes. I dimly sensed that I was trapped inside a conspiracy, a conspiracy that everyone else in the carriage was in on; it was all hopeless. I could either wait for the stewardess to come and scream at me again; or I could leave. I chose the latter. By the time I'd stood up, a middle-aged woman in a headscarf had slipped into my vacated seat. She was so quick, it was almost supernatural. When I looked back at her, she immediately rose half-heartedly and asked if I was planning to sit back down. Her flat, open face was so guileless that I couldn't believe she was behind this dastardly plot. I staggered over to the coupling of two carriages and leaned against a wall. Since there was no central heating and a significant draught, I had the space pretty much to myself. Even though it was a little chilly, I felt much more comfortable, much less oppressed than I had done back in the carriage. I even fell asleep briefly while standing up. I suddenly thought to go and check on my luggage but heard a strange squelching noise as soon as I took a step in its direction. Looking down, I discovered that I was standing in yet another puddle of water, trickling down onto the receding train tracks through a hole in the metal floor. I stamped my feet, almost ready to cry with agitation. After checking that no one was coming, I squatted down by the pool of clear water. I dipped my finger in and sniffed it. As it touched the water, I shivered; it was freezing cold, as if it had just run off a glacier. I thought absent-mindedly of my imaginary ice sculpture; had she started to melt on the journey down south? I could think of no other explanation. If I wanted to avoid seeping water all the way down to the Yangtze – and the inevitable social problems this would cause – I would have to forget her as fast as possible. She belonged to Harbin, hundreds of miles to the north; I couldn't take her home with me to Nanjing.

It was New Year's Eve by the time I got back to Nanjing. When the train passed Jinan in Shandong, I started to run a temperature; I could tell I was going to be properly ill. Eventually, I managed to stagger to Xiao Liu's, still carrying my three rotting cabbages. I had nowhere else to go; my college dormitory would have been shut. Xiao Liu – around whose mouth a ring of stress blisters had broken out – exclaimed with relief as soon as he saw me. When school broke up, I'd written a short letter to my parents, telling them that I wasn't coming home and that I wanted to use the holiday to carry out a 'survey of society' (that was the exact phrase I used – it was very fashionable at universities in the mid-to-late 1980s). By the time they got the letter, I was already on my way. If I'd applied to them in writing first, they would never have let me go. I hadn't told Xiao Liu either, because he would certainly have rung my mother. The moment they received the letter, my parents got on the phone to Xiao Liu, who immediately rushed to my dormitory but found the bird had already flown. Convinced that he was to blame for my flight, Xiao Liu belaboured himself repeatedly to my parents, confessing that he had paid me four hundred *yuan*. My migraine-ridden mother was very tough on Xiao Liu for giving me so much money; I was bound to get into trouble with it, she said. As a result of all this, when I resurfaced in everyone's lives, Xiao Liu first shouted at me for a while, then told me to hand over any money I still had on me, for safe keeping. He next went out to ring my parents and tell them I was fine, and with him. I spent that New Year at Xiao Liu's; for one thing, I wouldn't have got to my parents' in time (even if I'd been able to get a ticket), because they were a six or seven hours' bus-ride from Nanjing; for another, Xiao Liu didn't want my parents to know that I was ill. And so a particularly unmerry New Year was had by all in the Liu household. While I lay in a deep, feverish sleep, his wife – holding her nose – threw away my three faithful, decomposed pickled cabbages.

*

I probably need to insert a little detail here about my relationship with Xiao Liu. He was an old student of my mother's; not a particularly brilliant one, but hardworking and devoted. His middle school years coincided with the nadir in my family's fortunes. My father was under investigation (for alleged illicit dealings with foreigners, espionage, possession of a radio transmitter – that kind of thing) and my mother had been banished to a school in deepest rural China to teach physics. No one learnt anything much in the Cultural Revolution, and especially not in the countryside; it was hard enough to find anyone interested in either studying or teaching, and harder again for them to encounter each other. Xiao Liu originally came to us not to study, but to fulfil an important undercover mission. He had a crashingly bad class background himself because one of his ancestors had been a shopkeeper in the county town and his own skin was too fair (he was the only boy in the school who used vanishing cream, for which he was universally derided). The local Party branch had given him a chance to redeem himself by spying on my mother, who was suspected of being my spymaster father's top accomplice. The difficulty in advancing the investigation was that all the other teachers, students and political activists in the village were terrified of her; she didn't suffer anyone particularly gladly. So Xiao Liu decided to make a living sacrifice of himself and win some political credit by personally investigating her.

Our family was one of the very few at the time to have a transistor radio at home. Xiao Liu promptly dismantled it, hoping to discover the rumoured transmitter. Having scattered parts all over the house, he unsurprisingly proved unable to resassemble them, for which my mother ripped several strips off him (at that moment, he was not a radio obsessive; my mother hadn't yet turned him). He next confiscated our dusty piles of old newspapers, went through every back issue of the weekly digest *Reference News* and was delighted to discover two copies missing (which my father had obviously sold to overseas agents in exchange for foreign currency). His toughest assignment was to try and break our family's code. My parents were both from south Fujian, on the east coast, and spoke to each other in the local dialect. When my grandmother was still alive, we spoke nothing but Fujianese at home, because she didn't understand Mandarin. Fujianese sounds utterly foreign to speakers of other dialects of Chinese; as a result, we were accused of speaking in cipher. The instant my mother spoke a word of Fujianese, Xiao Liu would ask what it meant. When my mother was in an adequately good mood, she would tell him, and he would lovingly transcribe it in pinyin. More likely, though, my grandmother would chase him out of the door with a broom, as she might an impudent chicken; Xiao Liu would then report back to the Party leadership about how this Fujianese battleaxe was probably the real ringleader of this den of spies.

Unfortunately, his surveillance work only intensified the contempt in which he was held at school. I will say one thing for him, though: however savage my mother was to him, he just sat there, blushing scarlet, taking it. And as long as no one outside our family was looking, he would fetch water or coal for us.

As time passed, so did our misfortunes. Xiao Liu still often visited, no longer to spy on us, but to learn about radios, on which my mother had got him hooked. He'd got into it to begin with for pragmatic reasons: as his family background restricted his study opportunities, he thought he'd learn a skill and open a stall fixing radios. My mother disapproved: a young person should have more ambition, she said. She was actually quite a decent person, ready to forgive the past transgressions of anyone except my father. Xiao Liu, for his part, always felt guilty about what he'd done, and repaid her with absolute submissiveness. And as the years went by, we became convinced by the genuineness of his devotion. His own low point came when they started sending students off to labour in the fields; whenever he got the chance, he'd run back to our house, utterly filthy, to weep with the frustration of it. My mother would comfort and encourage him; she lent him books to read, and even persuaded her head teacher to let him have the waste from the school toilets for his production team. Eventually, my mother persuaded this same head teacher to transfer him back to the school as a temporary lab technician; this gave Xiao Liu the crucial time and conditions to make up the study he'd missed and make him believe in the possibility of a life built on knowledge. It was my mother again who made the head teacher find him a place to study in Nanjing. My mother had an extraordinary influence over this unlucky head teacher, because he happened also to be my father.

Xiao Liu was a ubiquitous presence through my childhood. When I was little, I'd sometimes go into these strange, staring trances, and wander blindly off. More often than not, it was Xiao Liu who brought me home again; my mother didn't trust anyone else to look after me. I was less keen on the arrangement: Xiao Liu's only talent, as far as I could see, was his ability to perform handstands, and even those weren't free-standing. He had to prop himself against a tree or a wall, and even then satisfaction was not guaranteed; he often fell over and hurt his neck. He did a handstand to jolly me out of every one of my sulks; he must have done 1,500 to 2,000 of them through my formative years. After I started school, my mother turned Xiao Liu into an academic role model for me. I later held Xiao Liu responsible for my parents forcing me to apply to Nanjing University. In the New Year's holiday of my third year at high school (he always came back from Nanjing, bearing gifts, to see my parents), he promised my mother that he would look after me if I went to university in the city. As the post-Mao thaw deepened, as their lives got easier in other ways, it was me, and not Maoist mass movements, who became the chief trigger of my mother's migraines; the idea of a common law guardian keeping an eye on me was a great comfort to her.

According to my understanding, Xiao Liu had precisely zero love life before the age of thirty. After that significant birthday, he finally – after submitting to various pressures and introductions – met short, dark, chubby Lin Zhimin. Unable to decide what to do about her, he took her on a long bus pilgrimage to see my parents, to get their view on the issue. After the lavish meal that my mother had cooked for them, Xiao Liu tiptoed into the kitchen to ask her what she thought of Lin Zhimin. Uncomfortable at the idea of taking responsibility for something so important, my mother muttered something formulaic about how she seemed a very nice girl.

'You don't like her, do you?' Xiao Liu frowned.

'Why do you say that?' my mother quickly replied.

'I can hear it in your voice,' he said. 'You don't talk like that if you really like a person.'

My mother tried to placate him with a change of tone: 'She seems a very nice girl.' And so it was, not long after their return to Nanjing, that Xiao Liu and Lin Zhimin registered their marriage. I was in my fifth year at primary school at the time, but I can still remember the wedding banquet clearly. I sat at one corner of a table, listening to the adults' conversation, staring at Lin Zhimin, because I had never seen a woman with so much nasal hair, and wondering where Xiao Liu had found her. Remembering dimly that Xiao Liu worked in the Soil Research Institute, and Lin Zhimin at the Irrigation Research Bureau, I decided to show off – as a complete non sequitur – by declaiming a term I'd just learned in geography: Soil Erosion. The adults at the table stared at me.

'What?' Xiao Liu asked. Thinking myself quite extraordinarily clever and well-informed, I explained the concept. My mother told me to shut up. Xiao Liu much later reminded me of this long-suppressed memory when he was casting around for long-term causes to explain the inevitability of his divorce. I couldn't quite confirm that I'd come out with such a casually damning prophecy, but I couldn't help wishing that I'd pronounced something more auspicious; perhaps if I'd said 'soil deposition' instead, things might have worked out better.

Not long after the divorce, Lin Zhimin remarried: this time, a bald doctor at the Workers' Hospital. They'd met when Lin Zhimin's right breast had developed a worrying swelling, which the doctor had carefully massaged away. The doctor came good for the family a second time, too. When Xiao Liu's son was in hospital with meningitis, this affable physician kept a close eye on him. Lin Zhimin said he was a distant relative on her mother's side, and Xiao Liu felt blessed indeed to have an in-law in the hospital. Later on, when his younger sister broke her leg, the doctor helped again; and even though Xiao Liu bought him thank you gifts, he still felt indebted. Unfortunately, this time the ending was less happy: the bone was not reset straight. Even today, when she tries to walk in a straight line, she finds herself going round in circles. This leg – with its out-turned knee – permanently soured Xiao Liu's feeling towards that period in his marriage, and also towards Lin Zhimin. After they separated, he did not allow Lin Zhimin, or her family, any contact with her son. I didn't hold any personal grudge against Lin Zhimin; while I was at university, I ate many meals cooked by her, and sometimes she even washed my quilt. But because of the way things had ended between her and Xiao Liu, I felt I had to hate her too, in solidarity. A few years ago, I bumped into her at the post office in the centre of Nanjing. She instantly blurted out a long stream of consciousness, most of it to do with Liu Gang and about how unreasonable Xiao Liu was being. She asked me to pass on to him that if he didn't let her see her son soon, she'd take him to the courts. Her face was noticeably more lined, due, I suspected, to her drastic weight loss. She looked transformed: she had a figure, a spark in her eyes. A neutral observer would say that she looked much better. This meeting set me thinking. I had to acknowledge that for Lin Zhimin, marriage to Xiao Liu had been rich in downsides – it had been an occurrence not unlike the swelling on her breast. I concluded that all women with swellings on their breasts should divorce. I also decided I wasn't going to hate her any more.

In all the years we've known each other, Xiao Liu and I have only had one argument, though it was a fairly serious one. It was in 1988, graduation year, and time to look for a job. I'd always wanted to go and work somewhere very far away, to get away from my parents, and especially my mother. (For years now, I'd had to make certain lifestyle sacrifices to mitigate her migraines). As my hopes for studying in Beijing had been squashed, I didn't want to lose the fresh opportunity that graduation offered to get some distance between the two of us. And at the time, universities were actually taking into account students' preferences before they assigned them jobs, which increased my chances of controlling my own destiny. On a visit to the Human Resources Exchange Centre, I discovered that the furthest away of the few work units taking graduates from my department was a new Thermal Electrics Company on Hainan, the tropical island dropped off China's south coast to which emperors used to exile their worst enemies. I went for it on the spot. As soon as I had handed in my form, I was hired. Now all I had to do was wait for my diploma to come through, and I was off. My mother – three hundred kilometres away – knew nothing of the particulars of what I'd been up to, but she intuited my desire to leave the southeast. It could be no coincidence that, soon after, Xiao Liu began regularly popping up in my dormitory to engage me in small talk about my future plans. Though I kept schtum, Xiao Liu made his own enquiries at the faculty office and, through a combination of threats and cajoling, managed to get me transferred back to Nanjing, which would be better for my mother's fragile nerves.

It was a busy time for Xiao Liu, that autumn. Even though he was under severe physical and mental pressure, he still spared the time to unravel the mess I'd got myself into. I cared nothing for that; my resentment at his intervention simmered away until it found an outlet. After graduation, at the height of the fierce Nanjing summer, Xiao Liu brought me boxes and string to pack up my things. I remembered that he was wearing an old white shirt and had a black mourning band around one of his short sleeves (his father had just died of cancer of the gall bladder). His face ran with sweat as he worked, his dust-covered shirt sticking to his body. Because of the stress he had been under, he had put on some weight. I stood there, gazing at his neck shuddering with rolls of fat, brooding on how my dreams had yet again been crushed. I suddenly exploded at him. I can't remember now exactly what I said, but probably what hurt him the most was my calling him a spy and an informer. He straightened up and gazed at me, open-mouthed, the colour slowly draining from his face. There he stood, silently shaking his head, until his eyes slowly filled with tears. I realised that I'd gone too far, but my room-mates were standing by, so I couldn't apologise. Finally, he set down his packing materials, brushed the dust off his hands and muttered that there was one more box left to tie up. He turned and left.

We didn't see each other for almost two years after that. In this time, I wrote him two, maybe three letters, hoping that he'd forgive me; he wrote one short reply, telling me he wasn't angry. He'd made a promise to my parents, which he'd fulfilled. Now I'd graduated, this responsibility was out of his hands and he no longer had to make me unhappy; I could choose my own way. Finally, he said he was very busy and wished me well in my career. I sensed that he had no desire to see me again. A few times I thought of going to see him, but when I considered how awkward such a meeting would be, I gave up on the idea. Although we were both in Nanjing, I worked in the north of the city, so there was little chance of us bumping into each other.

Our next meeting was at my parents,' one New Year. He'd brought his son and when my mother asked where Lin Zhimin was, he muttered something about her being too busy (by that point, they'd been separated some time). I noticed that his hair was much greyer than before and that he'd lost weight – it was particularly noticeable when he stood next to his son who, aged eight, was still pale and swollen from the steroids he'd been given when he was ill. You could tell that the boy knew he was not like other children. He had very little to say for himself; his eyes darted nervously about in their sockets; he hardly ate. The visit was very short – Xiao Liu didn't even stay for a meal – and the conversation naturally revolved around Liu Gang's misfortunes. Several times, Xiao Liu prodded Liu Gang's puffy face then watched as the indentation slowly sprang flat. He wanted to reassure my mother that it was fat, rather than just bloat. My mother was mainly worried about whether the illness had caused any cognitive damage. At the mere mention of this, Liu Gang sprinted out of the room and began chasing the family cat, which fled in terror. After this, Xiao Liu and I had a few meetings in Nanjing, all of which were initiated by me. I hoped that we could get back onto our old footing. He tried hard, too, and whenever we were together, an old, easy affection began to return between us, but if ever I tried to speak to him, about anything at all, this look of defensive reserve came over his face. I realised that some kinds of emotional damage could never be made good. So although we got on in a superficially normal way, we didn't tend to meet very often. Later on, I became more peripatetic, and for years did not return to Nanjing. So we were less and less likely to encounter each other.

It was at the end of last year that we started to see more of each other, thanks to a confluence of favourable circumstances. A decade had passed since my graduation, and time changes a person. Some things that once seemed very important become less so, while other things are sweetened with nostalgia. And no one made me tenderly nostalgic quite like Xiao Liu, now fifty and still nowhere near even a deputy departmental headship. In those ten years, my own life had changed; my insistence on doing things my own way had finally succeeded in entirely numbing my mother's neuroses. But the greatest change was that I no longer craved travel. After my eleven house moves and Xiao Liu's one, we ended up living only seven minutes' bike ride away from each other. We shopped at the same market, we bought liquid gas at the same depot; we couldn't avoid each other. Xiao Liu had not remarried, and his obsession with computers had given way to an obsession with his son. Liu Gang was now sixteen, but was only in the third year of elementary high. He was currently on his second (and not necessarily, his father felt, final) attempt at completing the year. Although very fat still, he was strong and tanned – an appealing physical presence. I was very fond of him, especially when he called me Uncle. Xiao Liu kept him on a short leash, which sometimes made their relationship rather edgy. I felt I'd been here before, with my mother. Because of my instinctive aversion to this parenting style, very often I couldn't stop myself intervening and managed to mitigate some of Xiao Liu's more draconian decisions. Liu Gang and I got on pretty well. When we were alone together, he had a lot to say for himself; it was only when his father was around that he clammed up. Strangely enough, sometimes if I said exactly the same thing that his father said, I would get a very different response. Xiao Liu happily let his son be influenced by me. Although he felt that things had been difficult for his generation, he was basically content with the way things had worked out. Now that he was fifty, he felt he was set on a certain course in life; but Liu Gang was still young. He could do better than his father (which, presumably, was where I came in). I suspected that Xiao Liu didn't know what sort of a person I really was. When we were together, it was mostly him doing the talking (he spoke of the Soil Research Institute as if it were the centre of the civilised world). I said very little about myself, not because I was deliberately concealing anything, but because I feared he might feel that my kind of life was an affront to his.

One evening, something occurred to me while we talked. After a couple of drinks too many at dinner, Xiao Liu sat on the shabby old sofa next to his bed, facing the eleven-inch black and white television that he had himself lovingly assembled years before. A group of girls who (allegedly) made their living from fishing suddenly began cavorting about on the screen, to express how ecstatic China's fisherpeople were about the whole reforms process. The sound was on so low you could hardly hear a thing, because Liu Gang was doing his homework in the sitting room, but I noted with surprise the way in which Xiao Liu's eyes were fixed almost greedily on the scene, as if he were ready to pluck one of the girls out of the television.

'Have you slept with anyone since you got divorced seven years ago?' I suddenly asked him. Xiao Liu slowly turned to face me (he had hyperplasia, second degree, of the cervical vertebra) and asked me to say it again; he hadn't caught it the first time.

He stood up when he'd heard the repeat, stared at me, then shot a question back, smiling defensively: 'What made you think of a thing like that?' Glancing uneasily at Liu Gang in the next-door room, he shut the door then returned to the sofa.

'Isn't it a normal, practical question to ask?' I said.

'Now that you put it like that,' Xiao Liu mumbled, looking at his feet, 'it does seem a good question.' After another while, he admitted to me that he hadn't.

I could hardly believe it: 'Not once, in seven years?' In fact, Xiao Liu confirmed, it was ten years, because he and Lin Zhimin had been separated three years before their divorce. I wasn't sure what to say next; in fact, I was regretting having brought the whole subject up and wondered how I could change it. Xiao Liu began smoking one of my cigarettes, squinting at me through the fumes (he'd never smoked in his life).

'When you call it ten years, it sounds a long time,' he went on, when I failed to say anything else, 'but it just didn't seem a big deal. It went by very quickly; I never even thought about it.' Now I wanted to change the subject even more badly than before, but Xiao Liu was just getting into his stride.

Going home that evening, I felt I shouldn't have let things get to this point. As my mother often said, Xiao Liu was a good person, it was just that he wasn't very in touch with his own feelings. He was like a spinning top – without a whip, he didn't know where to turn. He had looked out for me so many times; it was time for me to repay the favour. And so I urged him to place the search for a mate at the top of his list of priorities. From now on, I told him, he couldn't spend every day hiding in the Soil Research Institute. He had to get out more. There were a lot more places to look for a girlfriend than there used to be, what with Brides Firms and Singles Clubs; and even if he didn't get a result, at least it would be a change of scene. If he was embarrassed, I'd go with him; I had plenty of time on my hands. Intensely moved by my offer, Xiao Liu told me he wasn't worth bothering over at his age; he was quite happy watching women on the street when he went out shopping. I told him he wasn't too old: he had good skin and with a judicious touch of hair dye, he could look twenty years younger. I was telling him the truth, and I told him more than once. Then he used Liu Gang as an excuse: he was worried that his son wouldn't adjust, and in any case he was too busy keeping an eye on his schoolwork. I took the opposite view: one, I could talk to Liu Gang; two, if he had a wife, wouldn't it free up time to help Liu Gang? I refuted every excuse that Xiao Liu came up with, until he ran out of them and told me straight that he just didn't want to go through with it. When I pressed him about it, he got more and more adept at fobbing me off, and even went on the counteroffensive: Why hadn't I ever married? My parents were always ringing him about it, and so on. I told him not to change the subject. But just as you can't turn a determined suicide, you can't marry off a confirmed bachelor. Once Xiao Liu lost his temper with me: I'd never married, he told me, I had no idea what agony it was to live with the wrong woman. Find the right woman, I riposted.

'Easily said,' Xiao Liu rejoined, 'harder done. Anyway, who'd have me?' I asked him what kind of woman he actually wanted. 'Don't laugh at me,' he eventually blurted out, 'but someone just like your mother.' I was genuinely lost for words; I'd always thought that my father was the only man in the world who could put up with her. 'When we were at school,' Xiao Liu went on, 'everyone in my class was in love with her. We all thought she was our ideal woman.'

*

A few final words about the inspiration for this story. Early one morning last December, I had a dream. The afternoon before, on the fifth of the month, I'd fixed up to meet a friend at the Jiangsu Exhibition Centre in Nanjing, after which we were meant to be going to the People's Hospital to visit an older friend of ours, who was in for a cataract operation. I didn't mind when my friend kept me waiting as usual. I sat down on the barrier between the road and the pavement, studying the sky, the traffic, the girls going past. It's been a lifelong hobby of mine. But as I did so, I felt someone else was watching me, from behind. I didn't care to begin with; it seemed fair enough that an inveterate watcher should also be watched. But eventually, I turned around and discovered it was a young albino girl standing by a newspaper stall. Her hair and eyebrows were palest-blonde, her skin a pinkish gypsum-white, and scattered intermittently with light brown freckles. Her eyes – squinting in the sun – shone with a naked desire. When our eyes met, she immediately turned away and pretended to rearrange the magazines on the stall. On realising that I was still studying her, she fled into the crowd. I overheard an exchange between two people who saw her push by them. 'Was that a foreigner?' one was asking. 'No, an albino,' the other one snapped impatiently back. That evening, reading in bed, the whole scene came back to me, and I was sure that the memory generated the dream I had the following morning: I was following an old, crumbling wall along a lake at dusk, while a flock of birds rested on a tree growing out of a crack in the wall. I looked around me, wondering why the place was so deserted, when suddenly I spotted a girl staring at me. I recognised her as the half-Russian I'd seen all those years ago in Harbin. She hadn't changed at all, except for her sapphire eyes, which seemed to burn with a grievance I didn't remember from before – as if she was reproaching me for not having looked at her for so long, for not having thought of her. I realised that she was right: I hadn't thought of her for a decade – not even once. I should have done.

I should thank Xiao Liu for how clearly I recalled this dream, because his phone call woke me from it. He knew my rhythms and wouldn't usually ring me early in the morning unless there was an emergency. He wanted me to talk to Liu Gang as soon as I could. He had been rather secretive recently, and Xiao Liu was worried that he was in contact with his mother. So he'd tailed him for the past twenty-four hours, and had discovered instead that his son had been on a date with an equally overweight female classmate. Xiao Liu was almost insane with rage: he swore that if Liu Gang managed to finish school now, he'd eat his own head. Though I had no idea how I would go about it, I accepted my mission – what choice did I have?

About the Authors

Jie Chen is a graduate of the Sichuan Normal University, and is a former cultural journalist. A native of Chengdu, she has written for the *Chengdu Evening News*, and since 1995, for papers such as *Southern Metropolis Daily*, the *Beijing Morning Post* and the *Nanfang Daily*. Her novels are extremely popular and include *Burgundy Ice Blue*, *Poisoning*, which has been adapted into a TV series, and *I Love You, Bye*.

Born in 1960 in Shenyang in Liaoning Province, **Diao Dou** is currently editor of *Contemporary Review*. A graduate of the University of Broadcasting in Beijing, he worked as a journalist before turning to fiction. Having established himself with a collection of poems, he has since turned to short stories and novels.

Having been brought up in the countryide (owing to his parents being sent there during the Cultural Revolution), **Han Dong** taught Western Philosophy at a small college for some years, before becoming a full-time writer. Dong has been well-known since the 1980s as one of China's most important avant-garde poets and is now increasingly influential as an essayist, short story writer and novelist. Han's works include collections of poetry, essays, short stories, novellas, and four full-length novels. His novel *Banished!* won the Independent Chinese Language Media Novel Prize in 2003, and was long-listed for the Man Asia Literary Prize when translated.

Cao Kou was born in Nanjing in 1977. He is renowned for a simple and direct style of writing, plainly describing strange situations with far-reaching implications. Hailed as one of the most talented young contemporary authors, he has published several collections of short stories, including *Fuck, Like the Dead*, and *More and More*. He's also published works on the life of Saddam Hussein and the history of sexuality in China.

Born in 1966 in Shanghai, **Ding Liying** is one of a new generation of Chinese women writers. Acclaimed for her carefully crafted portraits of ordinary urban women, she is an essayist and poet, as well as a short story writer, and has recently translated the poetry of Elizabeth Bishop. She was awarded the Anne Kao Poetry Prize in 1999.

Ho Sin Tung was born in Hong Kong in 1986 and graduated from the Chinese University of Hong Kong with a Fine Arts degree in 2008. Ho is now a full-time artist based in Hong Kong, and occasionally writes for newspapers and magazines in Hong Kong and Taipei. Visit: htpp://hosintung.com

Zhu Wen was born in Fujian Province in 1967 and spent his childhood in Jiangsu. After graduating from Dongnan University with a degree in engineering, he worked for five years in a thermal power plant. He began publishing his poetry in 1989, and soon became associated with the Nanjing-based group of 'Tamen' poets, a loose affiliation that includes Han Dong, Xiao Wei and Li Hongqi, among others. He has published six collections of novellas and short stories, two collections of poetry and one novel. He first gained fame with his 1995 short story collection *I Love Dollars* (published by Penguin in 2010). He is also an accomplished screenwriter and director: his directorial debut *Seafood* won the Grand Jury Prize at the 2001 Venice Film Festival, and his second film *South of the Clouds* was awarded the NETPAC Prize at the 2004 Berlin Film Festival.

Yi Sha was born Wu Wenjian in Chengdu in 1966. He graduated from Beijing Normal University in 1989 with a major in Chinese and is currently lecturing at the Xi'an International Studies University. His poetry collections include *Starve the Poets!*, *The Bastard's Songs*, *I Finally Understood Your Rejection*, *Out-of-Body Experiences*, and *Bedwetting*. His essay collections include *Leading a Life of Debauchery by Force, Shameless are the Ignorant,* and *Morning Bell and Evening Drum.* His short story collections include *A Bliss Beyond the Ordinary* and *Whoever Hurts, Knows.* His novels include *The Gold in the Sky* and *Bewildered.*

Xu Zechen was born in 1978 in Jiangsu Province, and obtained a Masters degree in Chinese literature at Peking University. He is currently editor at *People's Literature* magazine. Despite this pedigree, Xu's fiction is focused primarily on China's less-fortunate social classes – peddlers of pirated DVDs, migrant workers – and his spare, realist style lends some wry humour to their struggles. Xu has published three novels, *Midnight's Door*, *Night Train* and *Heaven on Earth*, and a collection of short stories entitled *How Geese Fly up to Heaven.* He has won several prizes within China for new and promising writers, and is generally considered one of the burgeoning new stars of China's literary scene.

Zhang Zhihao was born in the autumn of 1965 in Jingmen, Hubei Province, and now lives in Wuhan. He was chief editor of the large poetry volume *Poems of the Han.* His principal works include the poetry collections, *Suffering from Praise, Animal Heart* and *The Warmth of Collision*, the short fiction collection, *Going to See the People in the Zoo*, and the novels, *Trying to Coexist with Life, The Celestial Construction Team* and *Where the Water Ends.* His award-winning work has been included in several annual anthologies.

About the Translators and Editors

Eric Abrahamsen has lived in Beijing since 2001, when he studied Chinese at the Central University for Nationalities. He is a literary translator and publishing consultant, and one of the founders of Paper-Republic.org, a website promoting Chinese literature abroad. He is the recipient of PEN and NEA translation grants, and most recently translated Wang Xiaofang's novel *Notes of a Civil Servant* for Penguin.

Yu Yan Chen is a poet and translator based in New York. Her poetry collection *Small Hours* was published by the New York Quarterly in 2011. She specialises in translating contemporary Chinese fiction and poetry into English.

Liu Ding (Ed.) was born in 1976, in Changzhou Jiangsu Province, China. His first solo exhibition was in 1998 in Nanging, after which he Established Pink Studio Space. He's a founder member of the Complete Art Experience Project, and from 2007-2008 was Artistic Director of JoyArt, Beijing. His work has been exhibited in China, Sweden, Berlin, Germany, Italy, Russia, the UK and Switzerland. He currently lives and works in Beijing as an independent artist.

Nicky Harman's translations include Zhang Ling's prize-winning novel *Gold Mountain Blues*, Xinran's *Message from Unknown Chinese Mothers*, and Xinran's *China Witness* (with Esther Tyldesley and Julia Lovell). She is active on the literary website, Paper-Republic.org, and has been Translator-in-Residence at the Free Word Centre, London. She has also recently edited *A Phone Call from Dalian* (Zephyr Press), a selection of translated poems by Han Dong.

Rachel Henson's formative experiences in Chinese include training in the Woman Warrior Role in Beijing and touring a cabaret show around Chinese cities. She has written Chinese teaching materials for UK universities and worked on Chinese arts projects for the British Council, the Royal Court Theatre and the British Museum.

Brendan O'Kane lives in Beijing, where he works as a freelance writer and translator. He's also one of the hosts for *Popup Chinese*, a Chinese-learning podcast, reviews of which have described him as 'only slightly annoying.'

Julia Lovell teaches modern Chinese history at Birkbeck College, University of London. She is the author of *The Politics of Cultural Capital*, *The Great Wall: China Against the World* and *The Opium War: Drugs, Dreams and the Making of China*. Her many translations of modern Chinese fiction include Han Shaogong's *A Dictionary of Maqiao*, Zhu Wen's *I Love Dollars*, and Lu Xun's *The Real Story of Ah-Q, and Other Tales of China*.

Carol Yinghua Lu (Ed.) was born in Guangdong, in 1977. She studied English Literature at the Sun Yat-sen University, Guangzhou, and Malmo Art Academy, Sweden. One of China's most active and dynamic curators and critics, Carol was on the selection panel for the 2011 Golden Lion Award at the Venice Biennale and is one of the Co-Artistic Directors of the 2012 Gwangju Biennale. Carol regularly writes for a number of journals including *Frieze*, *Contemporary* and *Today Art* and is co-editor of *Contemporary Art & Investment* magazine. Her recent curatorial work includes 'The Temperament of Detail' at the Red Mansion Foundation, London, 'Foreign Objects' at the Project Space of Kunsthalle Wien in Vienna, 'The Weight of Reality' in Marella Gallery, Beijing, and 'There is No Story to Tell — An Exhibition of International Artists' at Tang Contemporary, Beijing.

Ra Page (Ed.) is the founder of Comma Press.

Petula Parris-Huang has translated a number of short stories from Chinese. She previously served as an in-house translator to the Taiwanese government and a lecturer in translation at the University of Bath. Petula holds an MA in Interpreting and Translating and a BA in Chinese with Russian.

Josh Stenberg has translated two collections of Su Tong's shorter fiction, *Madwoman on the Bridge and Other Stories* (2008) and *Tattoo: Three Novellas* (2010). He is a Lecturer at Nanjing Normal University and a PhD candidate in Chinese Theater at Nanjing University.

Special Thanks

The publishers would like to thank the following people without whom the logistical challenges of delivering this book would have been too much: Jon Fawcett of the British Library, Nicholas Chapman and Judith Luedenbach at the British Council, Joel Martinsen, Ying Kwok, Kate Griffin, Jo Lusby at Penguin China, Cathy Bolton at Manchester Literature Festival, Tianshu Zhang for her translation assistance, Philip Dodd, Trudi Shaw, and in particular Anna Holmwood.

We would especially like to thank our funders and creative partners, Alison Boyle at Arts Council England, and Lucy Yang, Katie Popperwell and Karen Wang at the Confucius Institute at the University of Manchester.

Madinah

CITY STORIES FROM THE MIDDLE EAST
ED. JOUMANA HADDAD

978-1905583072
£7.95

Featuring:
Nedim Gursel (Istanbul), Nabil Sulayman (Latakia), Joumana Haddad (Beirut), Ala Hlehel (Akka), Gamal Al-Ghitani (Alexandria), Yitzhak Laor (Tel Aviv), Elias Farkouh (Amman), Yousef Al-Mohaimeed (Riyadh), Fadwa Al-Qasem (Dubai), and Hassan Blasim (Baghdad).

'Madinah' – the Arabic word for 'city' – may conjure labyrinthine streets and the hustle and bustle of the souq in Westerners' minds, but for the inhabitants of the Middle East it is a much more mercurial thing, one that's changing today faster than ever.

Here – in ten urban stories set across the region – the city reveals itself through a vibrant array of characters: from the celebrated author collecting an award in the city that exiled him decades before, to the forlorn lover waiting at a rendezvous as government officials raid nearby shops, confiscating 'wanton' Valentine's Day roses.

For all we think we know of the conflict and exoticism of the region, nothing opens more doors to what we don't than its writing. Here, ten short stories by new and established writers have been selected and translated into English for the first time, to open just such a door...

www.commapress.co.uk

Decapolis

TALES FROM TEN CITIES
ED. MARIA CROSSAN

978-1905583034
£7.95

Featuring:
Larissa Boehning (Berlin), David Constantine (Manchester), Arnon Grunberg (Amsterdam), Emil Hakl (Prague), Amanda Michalopoulou (Athens), Empar Moliner (Barcelona), Aldo Nove (Milan), Jacques Réda (Paris), Dalibor Šimpraga (Zagreb), Ágúst Borgþór Sverrisson (Reykjavik).

Decapolis is a book which imagines the city otherwise. Bringing together ten writers from across Europe, it offers snapshots of their native cities, freezing for a moment the characters and complexities that define them. Ten cities: diverse, incompatible, contradictory – in everything from language to landscape.

'Europe is heavy with history and the trace left by cataclysm and upheaval. These are present in these tales, and yet coexist with a kind of wry and knowing playfulness.'
– A.S. Byatt in *The Times*

'The European short story is clearly in vigorous form.'
– Matthew Sweet, *Nightwaves, Radio 3*

'A fine, streetwise cacophony'
– *The Independent*

www.commapress.co.uk

Beijing – Chengdu – Guangzhou – Harbin – Hong Kong – Nanjing –
Shanghai – Shenyang – Wuhan – Xi'an

*'Everyone in the whole country knew this place was full of money, you only
had to bend down and pick it up; everyone in the whole country also knew
that opportunity here was like bird shit – while you weren't looking it would
spatter on your head and make you rich...'*

To the West, China may appear an unstoppable economic unity, a single
high-performing whole, but for the inhabitants of this vast, complex and
contradictory nation, it is the cities that hold the secret to such economic
success. From the affluent, Westernised Hong Kong to the ice-cold Harbin
in the north, from the Islamic quarters of Xi'an to the manufacturing
powerhouse of Guangzhou - China's cities thrum with promise and
aspiration, playing host to the myriad hopes, frustrations and tensions
that define China today.

The stories in this anthology offer snapshots of ten such cities, taking in as
many different types of inhabitant. Here we meet the lowly Beijing mechanic
lovingly piecing together his first car from scrap metal, somnambulant
commuters at a Nanjing bus-stop refusing to acknowledge the presence
of a dead body just metres away, or Shenyang intellectuals conducting a
letter-writing campaign on the moral welfare of their city. The challenges
depicted in these stories are uniquely Chinese, but the energy and ingenuity
with which their authors approach them is something readers everywhere
can marvel at.

Jie Chen - Han Dong - Diao Dou - Cau Kou - Ding Liying
Ho Sin Tung - Yi Sha - Zhu Wen - Xu Zechen - Zhang Zhihao

£9.99
Comma Press
www.commapress.co.uk
Design by David Eckersall
Cover image: 'Street - Haizhu Square' by Chen Shaoixong

9 781905 583461 >

Supported by the
Confucius Institute at the
University of Manchester.